"I need to know you
know what to cry o

"And I need to know yours,'
the beautiful woman beside him a light nip on
the neck. "So I know who now owns me body
and soul."

She stretched out lethargically and kissed his
jaw. Then, lifting a shoulder, she allowed the
robe to fall completely off one arm. As he bent
lower to taste that sweet, smooth skin, she
whispered, "My name's—"

Before she could finish, the door opened,
and a light flashed on. "It's J.T.," Nate said.
"Oh, boy."

"Oh, boy is right," the woman echoed, her
horror undisguised.

Nate shifted slightly to the side, hiding her
behind him, as J. T. Birmingham entered the
room.

Taking stock of the situation—and not looking
the least bit surprised—J. T. finally said, "Son,
I think you're wearing my robe."

Nate groaned. He'd been caught by a
millionaire, wearing the man's robe during
an important cocktail party at which he was
the guest of honor. Caught fooling around with
a gorgeous stranger on that man's trampoline.
"Can things get any worse?" he muttered.

"And," J.T. continued, "you're lying on top of
my daughter...."

Dear Reader,

I love Broadway musicals. And I've always been fascinated by the thought of looking across a crowded room on "one enchanted evening" and finding a stranger who turns your world upside down. That's exactly what happens to my heroine, columnist Lacey Clark, who falls instantly for a devastatingly attractive man during a crowded party. When she finds herself alone with him a few moments later— and they end up naked on top of a trampoline—she never imagines that she's in the arms of her nemesis, Nate Logan.

Can two enemies-turned-lovers navigate the rocky road to romance in the sometimes outrageous world of magazine publishing? I sure had fun finding out while writing *Into the Fire.*

Those of you who read my first Temptation novel, *Night Whispers,* will recognize some characters in this book. I was so happy to find just the right story for Kelsey Logan's older brother, and I got a kick out of writing more of those sexy radio show segments. For my readers who have written to me asking for a sequel…I hope this one lives up to your expectations.

I'd love to hear what you think. Please drop me a line at P.O. Box 410787, Melbourne, FL 32941-0787, or write to me through my Web site: www.lesliekelly.com.

Enjoy,

Leslie Kelly

Books by Leslie Kelly

HARLEQUIN TEMPTATION
747—NIGHT WHISPERS
810—SUITE SEDUCTION
841—RELENTLESS

INTO THE FIRE
Leslie Kelly

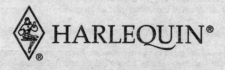

HARLEQUIN®

TORONTO • NEW YORK • LONDON
AMSTERDAM • PARIS • SYDNEY • HAMBURG
STOCKHOLM • ATHENS • TOKYO • MILAN • MADRID
PRAGUE • WARSAW • BUDAPEST • AUCKLAND

With love to the Smith kids:
Lynn, Donna, Karen, Cheri and Lee.
I can't think of five other people I'd rather have
grown up with—telephone poles and all.

ISBN 0-373-25972-7

INTO THE FIRE

Copyright © 2002 by Leslie Kelly.

1

ALONE in a throng of elegantly dressed people, in the lavishly appointed reception room of a tasteful Baltimore mansion, Lacey Clark began to sweat. Not a ladylike beading of perspiration on her upper lip. Not a moistness at her temple. No. Her tight black cocktail dress was growing downright damp as each additional person oozed into the already overcrowded party. A few more minutes and there would be circles under her armpits and her makeup would run off her skin in great bisque streaks.

"Get me out of here," she murmured, wondering if she could make it through the sea of people to the exit. Surely no one would notice if she slipped away. After all, she looked like practically every other woman in the place. Ninety percent of the females at the party wore the typical city social uniform—a little black cocktail dress, sheer black stockings, shiny, never seamed. Ridiculously high heels, useless tiny bag barely big enough to carry a tube of lipstick. Not to mention the confident expression disguising boredom.

Boredom *always* made Lacey Clark sweat. As did low-cut, skintight dresses and heels so high she wondered if she was going to fall on her fanny and humiliate herself in front of Baltimore society. Not that she really cared about Baltimore society. This was definitely *not* her crowd. Lacey would much rather have been at her favorite bar with her best friends.

For the hundredth time, she wished she'd been able to find a way out of this evening's event. As if it wasn't bad enough that her dress was uncomfortably tight, her stockings scratchy and her makeup oozy, her entire *life* was about to change course. Lacey didn't like feeling cornered nor having her personal affairs made very, *very* public. And tonight, in her boss's home, at a cocktail party where she was about to be honored for her job, she was also about to be set up for some major intrusion into her personal life. Her family. Her history. Her nice, orderly world.

"Dammit," she whispered, knowing things were completely beyond her control and not liking it one bit.

Nearby, two senior staff members from the magazine where she worked beckoned her closer. She smiled and pointed over her shoulder, implying she was waiting for someone. She didn't want to engage in small talk. Lacey just wanted to escape.

It might be possible to slip away for a few minutes, but she couldn't get away entirely, not when she was scheduled to receive a very public award for a job well done. Besides, even if she did disappear, J.T. Birmingham, millionaire publisher and owner of *For Her Eyes Only*, the magazine Lacey worked for, would make his second announcement anyway. The big one. The personal one. The one that would reveal beyond a doubt the intimate connection between them that she'd struggled to keep quiet.

Nothing she'd said in the past six weeks had dissuaded him. He was bursting at the seams, and he wanted the world in on his jubilation. Never mind that Lacey didn't.

No, a dash for the door was out. But she could at least hide for a while. She tried to sidle toward the exit but hadn't gone three steps when a voice stopped her.

"Did you see his new column?"

Lacey didn't even have to turn around. She knew who was speaking—her good friend Raul Santos. She certainly knew who he was speaking about. Nate Logan. Yuck.

The open door still taunted her from across the room. She stared at it longingly, knowing it offered an avenue of escape, a minute of peace and quiet, a chance to find a hidden corner and wipe the sweat off her forehead with the back of her arm. Stopping meant frustration. No question about it.

She muttered a curse and turned. "I don't read his column." Lacey stepped closer to Raul, who had worked with her at *For Her Eyes Only* magazine until a few months before. "Besides, I can count on you to tell me what was in it, right?"

A wide white smile creased Raul's darkly tanned face, enhancing his sharply attractive features. "Of course. You know, if I'd realized I was going to have this much fun being a double agent, reporting back and forth between the two of you, I would have taken the job at *Men's World* for much less money!"

"No, you wouldn't," she retorted with a smirk. "You need the money to keep up with the women."

"I would have forgone even that if I'd thought you really wanted me to stay." Raul smiled again, a glitter in his dark brown eyes. "You look exceptionally beautiful tonight, Lacey."

"Knock it off. We're way past that," she snarled.

No question, Raul was definitely *hot*, in a lean and lanky Latin lover way. But since they'd first met as lowly grunts at the magazine, they'd recognized they were destined to be friends, particularly since Raul was three years younger than Lacey. She looked at him like he was one of her little brothers, which he claimed wounded his male ego nearly beyond repair. Still, Raul couldn't help flirting. It was his modus operandi.

"So, you didn't see it?"

"No. Are you going to tell me?"

He paused as if debating it. A definite act since she knew he got a kick out of the fiery feud between Lacey and her nemesis, columnist Nate Logan who wrote for *Men's World.* "Well, he *does* expect me to," he finally said.

Lacey frowned. "Most double agents don't go around bragging about playing from both sides of the deck."

"Oh, I'm lousy at keeping secrets. Remind me to tell you what he said when I told him you called him a pimply prepubescent boy trapped in a man's body."

She groaned. "Raul..."

"Okay. In the column this month, he talks about a certain unnamed female magazine columnist who's either a man-hating femi-Nazi or a frigid virgin."

"What?" she shrieked, drawing the attention of those nearby. She immediately lowered her voice. "That son of a..."

"Well, Lacey, you did take a serious shot in your last column. Come on, saying all men who go to nightclubs are cheats looking to score?"

"Aren't they?"

"They're not all cheats."

"But they're all looking to score!"

"Then you went on to mention *certain* men who enjoy being photographed in such clubs surrounded by brainless bimbos."

"I didn't mention him by name."

"You didn't have to, darling, the whole country, let alone the city of Baltimore, knows the two of you have a private war going on."

She couldn't deny that. It was entirely true. Somehow, she, Lacey Clark, had gotten caught up in a battle of the sexes with a man she'd never met, never even laid eyes on, except for one grainy photo in a social rag. Even then she hadn't been able to see much of him since he'd been photographed wearing a Panama hat, dark glasses and holding a big, ugly cigar between his teeth.

Besides, she hadn't been able to look too closely at the photo considering all the breasts. The man had been photographed framed on all sides by women's breasts. Proudly. He'd been sitting in a chair while buxom beauties all around him showed just why they'd been finalists in the bar's wet T-shirt contest, which he'd judged. *Sexist pig.*

She shook her head, forcing thoughts of Nate Logan out of her mind. Tonight, as strange as it seemed considering he had been driving her nuts for months, he was the absolute least of her problems. If it meant keeping J.T. from revealing the truth about Lacey to the entire world, heck, she'd get up on stage and dance the tango with the man! It wouldn't, though. J.T. was determined. So she got to deal with the two biggest anxieties in her life on the very same night. J.T. And Nate Logan.

Resigned, she asked, "Is Logan here yet?"

Raul grinned, obviously knowing she couldn't restrain her curiosity. It was hell never having seen your publicly sworn enemy! "Holding court outside, last time I checked," Raul said.

"Great. Maybe we'll get lucky and one of his bimbos will drag him off to a frat party."

"Probably be more fun than here."

Lacey grinned reluctantly. "Yeah, you're probably right. Ah, for the simple days. Games of quarters until you passed out, staggering into class for an exam after an all-nighter."

Raul raised a brow. "Lacey Clark, Miss In-Control, playing quarters at a frat house? People'd pay money to see that."

She shrugged, then sighed. No, most people wouldn't be able to grasp that mental image. Not with the Lacey they knew now. The Lacey *most* people knew now.

Raul obviously noticed the smile fade from her lips. "My car's out back. Wanna run away and find the nearest bar?"

"You know I can't."

"I know," he admitted. "J.T.'s still going to do it?"

Lacey nodded.

"Okay, then, we're stuck. But I know you're bored outta your skull. If we have to stay, we can at least stir up some trouble. You know you're just dying inside to go up to Norm Spencer's wife and tell her everyone in the room can see the line of her girdle because her dress is too small."

"She either needs a better girdle or a dress two sizes bigger," Lacey admitted.

"That's my girl."

Lacey shook her head. "You're so bad."

"Maybe that's why we get along so well." Raul's eyes glittered. "Birds of a feather..."

"Get shot down together? No, I have to behave myself."

Raul gave her a gentle squeeze on one shoulder. "That's the problem, doll face. You keep trying so hard to be good, one day you're gonna just explode."

Before Lacey could toss off a reply—feeling the need to assure him that being good was more effort than instinct—her attention was drawn to the bar where one man in a sea of black tuxedos stood out. Around her, conversations continued to drone on, but the voices and high-pitched laughter faded to an indistinguishable buzz. Lacey suddenly found herself tense and aware for the first time this evening.

"Who's he?" she wondered aloud, not really directing the question at Raul, though he stood beside her.

"Who?"

Lacey didn't reply, still studying the man. She didn't stare because he was gorgeous, though he was. He didn't catch her eye because he filled out his tux better than any other man in the room, though he did. No, it was his obvious boredom that caught her attention. His looks merely *kept* it.

He was taller than average, long and lean. His dark blond hair was thick and wavy, and she imagined his wife or girlfriend would be unable to keep her fingers out of it. The way he held his body screamed self-confidence.

She wasn't the only one who noticed him. Lacey watched a curvy redhead approach the bar, try to strike up a conversation, then walk away in a pique. The man shrugged and kept talking to the bartender. His boredom radiated toward her from across the room. He barely looked at the crowd surrounding him, instead giving all his attention to the guy making drinks.

The lean, strong line of his jaw made her wonder, suddenly, what color his eyes were. And whether his mouth was really as impossibly gorgeous as it appeared to be from over here. When he laughed in response to something the bartender said, Lacey sucked in a breath. Yes, the man had one heck of a mouth.

"The guy at the bar?" Raul asked, narrowing his eyes as he noticed her interest. "Not your type, Lace."

"So, you do know him?"

"In passing. And I'm afraid he wouldn't do for you."

"Why not? What's wrong with him?"

"He's a bonehead, Lacey. A jock with a Jaguar. Not a brain in his head. Got where he is on his looks."

"Oh, great." She sighed. "A Nate Logan type, you mean?"

Raul snorted a laugh. "Well, he's maybe not *that* bad. But definitely not someone you'd be interested in."

Too bad. It had been a long time since Lacey had looked at a man and felt such a sudden, overwhelming attraction. When she thought about it, she didn't think she'd *ever* gone breathless and jittery just from spying a stranger across a room.

Of course, she was a woman and she could appreciate a good-looking man. This one had looks to spare. But as her eyes kept returning to him, she knew it was more than looks. There was such power in his masculinity, such magnetism in his self-confidence. It was damned unfair for a creature so breathtakingly male not to have the brains to go with the rest of the package. "What a shame," she murmured as she forced herself to look away.

"True," Raul replied.

Raul chuckled again, and Lacey wondered if he was up to something. She didn't quite trust the humor in his eyes. "What?"

"I'm thinking how fortunate it is," he said with a Raulish smirk, "that beauty isn't always wasted on the stupid." He pointed to himself.

Lacey laughed. Despite the arrogance and oozy charm, Raul was loyal, smart and a real friend. "Thanks for the tip, Raul."

"Logan's response to the prepubescent boy remark was..."

"I don't want to know," she said as she turned to leave. Hearing Raul's chuckle behind her, she knew he'd get around to telling her sooner or later.

As she walked toward the door, she did pause once to glance over her shoulder toward the bar. Though she told herself she was merely looking over the crowd, she still felt a pang of disappointment that the gorgeous blond hunk was no longer standing there. She looked around the room, but didn't spot him anywhere. "Just as well," she said with a sigh.

Lacey managed to fend off conversational gambits from several people as she eased across the room toward the exit. Some didn't try to talk to her, obviously seeing by the glint in her eye she was in no mood to chat. "Frigid virgin, indeed," she muttered, remembering what Raul had told her before she'd been so thoroughly distracted by the blond man.

She shouldn't have been surprised by the latest insult. Ever since the first shot in this war had been fired, nearly a year ago, she and that brainless, oversexed *Animal House* reject Nate Logan had traded barely veiled insults on the pages of *For Her Eyes Only* and *Men's World* every single month.

As the featured love-and-relationships columnists for their respective magazines, they should have had a lot in common, particularly since both magazines were owned by the same publisher, J.T. Birmingham. But they obviously had about as much in common as dirt and ice cream.

Nate Logan touted flirtation, sexual freedom, openness and exploration. He also liked to blame women for everything wrong with the male-female relationship. Lacey, on the other hand, knew darn right well it was usually the man who screwed things up on the romance front.

She also favored true love, soul mates and sexual responsibility. Hadn't her childhood, her entire life, been a never-ending lesson in that regard? With her mother's past and her stepfather's attitudes, Lacey had learned at a very young age that sexual mistakes could shatter lives. Heaven knew her stepfather had never let any of her family forget that lesson. She'd also decided—more out of a need for it to be true than anything else—that true love *had* to exist and was worth waiting for. She would settle for nothing else.

"Having a nice time, Lacey?" someone asked as she finally made it to the foyer of the mansion.

Seeing a colleague from work, Lacey forced a smile. "Yes. My favorite way to spend an evening." *Second only to having my bikini line waxed or my nails ripped out with hot pincers.*

"I hear you're going to receive some kind of award tonight," the woman continued.

Ah, yes, the award. The reason everyone thought they were at this party. If that were the only reason for tonight's gathering, Lacey would probably be able to relax and at least make a small effort to enjoy herself.

"And Nate Logan is, too," the woman continued, a note of maliciousness obvious in her tight smile.

"So I hear," Lacey muttered. She moved away, as if going to the powder room down the hall. If one more person stopped her and mentioned Nate Logan's name, she might have to throw up.

Lacey couldn't recall how her war with the other journalist had started. Who had lobbed the first insult? All she knew was last year she'd heard J.T. had hired a new columnist to spice up *Men's World*. Within three months, the magazine's formerly health-conscious, "strong mind, strong body" image had changed. It now appealed to the man who would rather be reading *Playboy* but had to mollify his wife or girlfriend by picking up a health magazine. So the centerfolds were somewhat clothed and usually reclining on exercise equipment or the hoods of automobiles.

She had to assume Nate's column, which had gained instant popularity, was part of the reason circulation had skyrocketed.

Seeing no one waiting outside the powder room, Lacey walked right past it, down a long corridor. When she heard voices in a nearby room, she ducked behind a piece of pricey statuary. Hearing the voices recede, she dashed by the doorway, trying to stay on her toes to avoid letting her heels click on the floor.

"Hide and seek," she whispered, knowing she was probably being juvenile and not really caring.

It wasn't just the aura of sex appeal on every page of *Men's World* that bothered her. She also didn't like Nate Logan's smart-ass tone, his flirtatious, irreverent writing style. She certainly didn't like his advice. But his readers obviously adored him. He'd even been given an unprecedented second column, "Nate's Notes on the Nice and the Naughty."

"Notes from Nate the Nitwit," she muttered sourly.

She had to admit that she'd been somewhat amused by his observations. But when he'd started getting a little too obnoxious, she'd reacted. She was only human, after all. Since he seemed to delight in targeting her sex, well, what else could a fair-minded woman do but defend herself?

Once, he wrote a column about the way women couldn't keep secrets. His theory was that a woman didn't make a single decision regarding career, life, love or sex without consulting her gaggle of girl-friends. He went on to use as an example the way women went to the ladies' room together at restaurants. His assertion? They were flipping a coin to see which one would sleep with her date and which would come down with a headache.

That, probably, was the first time Lacey had responded on the pages of *For Her Eyes Only*. She'd fired a mild shot about the way men felt it necessary to touch each others' butts during athletic events.

The battle had gone on from there. He'd claimed women's so-called emotional loyalty to each other disappeared whenever three females were together, since as soon as one left the other two dissed her awful shoes, tight dress or bad hairdo. Lacey retorted that the buddy syndrome was the way men got close to other men's girlfriends in order to hit on them.

He said women sent mixed signals, demanding equality yet having a fit and refusing sex if a man didn't always pick up the check for dinner. She said women wanted to be treated with respect, courtesy and graciousness, not like walking sex toys.

He said women drove men out with their demands. She said men walked out wide-eyed when a good set of legs happened along. He said women were untrustworthy. She said men were dogs.

He said. She said.

On and on the Ferris wheel turned in their undeclared war between the sexes. Their readers followed along in amusement, driving up circulation, ad revenues and publicity.

Lacey and Nate Logan had been invited to appear together on a nationally televised morning show. Lacey had refused, as always being careful to guard her privacy. She wouldn't have gone anyway. Sharing a magazine rack with Nate Logan was bad enough. Sharing a TV stage would be impossible.

If Lacey hadn't been too excited about her sudden notoriety, J.T. and the other higher-ups had been absolutely thrilled. So here they were, about to be toasted, *together*, by the publisher of both magazines they worked for.

"Unfair," she muttered as she made a few turns, passing J.T.'s private office and his wife's art studio. Lacey wasn't ready for this evening.

She could admit that it wasn't really the Nate Logan situation. The main problem tonight was the personal issue. The issue of Lacey Clark—who she really was, where she'd really come from. She'd pleaded with J.T. not to go ahead with the announcement he planned to make at the party. Not unexpectedly, he'd ignored her, caring only about the circulation numbers, not about personal feelings. Not even hers.

Lacey's high heels clicked loudly on the polished floor as she walked toward her destination. There was one spot where she knew she could be alone. She couldn't escape the inevitable forever. But she could at least take some time to prepare for the evening she faced.

Thirty minutes. She deserved thirty minutes of peace before J.T. changed her secure, comfortable, low-key world forever.

"NOTE TO SELF. Next time you attend a rich man's cocktail party, bring your Game Boy."

Nate Logan clicked off his microcassette recorder and tucked it into the pocket of his black tux. Since everyone he worked with knew he always carried the thing around with him, making observations for use in columns, no one would have been surprised to see him talking to himself. Not that it mattered, anyway, since he was alone. Completely, blissfully alone.

He'd finally cut out of J.T. Birmingham's party after enduring about twenty-five minutes of insipid conversation with colleagues who'd love to see him fall flat on his face. Grabbing a few bottles of beer from the bar, he'd slipped out a patio door and made his way around the lawn, searching for a place to sit down and drain a cold one.

Nate's exploration of the well-manicured grounds led him to a secluded pool area. The pool ran right up to the edge of the house, and he imagined there was another section inside for bad-weather swimming. Curious to see what it looked like, he tested the handle of a nearby door and found himself inside a recreation room, complete with gym and spa. A light in a far corner illuminated some pricey workout equipment, including weight-training centers, stair steppers, treadmills, even a trampoline. The enclosed pool took up the other half of the massive chamber.

"The magazine business must be doing very well, indeed," he mused as he moved a lounge chair right up to the edge of the pool. He took a seat, then leaned over the armrest to test the water with his fingers, liking the coolness against his skin. Damn, it was a miserably hot night, particularly for early June. The crowded party had made it that much more so.

He twisted off the cap of a bottle, took a long pull of cold beer and settled back in the chair. He would have loosened the stupid bow tie at his neck but knew there was no way he'd be able to tie it again without a mirror, so he left it alone.

All in all, the evening was proving to be a total waste. Hobnobbing with the rich and famous of Baltimore was not exactly Nate's thing. Most of the women he'd met tonight either stared icicles or came at him with enough heat to melt iron, each thinking she might be the one to transform the sexist bad boy she knew from the pages of *Men's World*.

As if that Nate Logan really existed.

Well, okay, maybe he existed to some extent. Yes, Nate's writing style reflected his personality—a little smart-alecky, a lot tongue in cheek. But the rest didn't. As much as readers—and female columnists—might argue it, Nate was not a sexist jerk. He didn't dislike women. Far from it! So he didn't particularly care to be exposed to a bunch of female readers who wanted to either smack him or seduce him.

It wasn't as if he bashed women. He wrote a column for men in a men's magazine. When he wrote, he pictured himself just talking to a bunch of guys. All guys—single or married, committed or on the make, young and eager or old and reminiscent—talked about women. What women did. What women said. What women wore. What women wanted. Particularly what women wanted. Mainly how the hell a man was supposed to figure out what women wanted!

He viewed his writing as a just-between-us-men, talking-after-a-workout kind of thing. Unfortunately, some women had started eavesdropping on the conversation and weren't too happy about it. As if he, Nate Logan, had invented the concept of men griping about the opposite sex. Ridiculous, unless one also subscribed to the theory that women never indulged in man bashing. Which was, of course, complete bullshit.

This was where his startlingly sudden success in the publishing world had gotten him. A great job, a terrific salary, the freedom to express the views of the average man on the street. Oh, and a big, fat, pig-shaped target on his head.

He didn't like his sudden notoriety. Sure, he'd had fun with it the first few months, until he realized not everyone was in on the joke. Some people didn't see the real Nate Logan at all anymore. He found himself on guard with each person he met, judged by other people's preconceptions. He'd begun to miss the anonymity he'd enjoyed working as a staff writer for a weekend magazine in D.C. or doing his freelance work. He'd rather be covering another corruption scandal in the nation's capital than be stuck here, at a highbrow party, surrounded by men who agreed with every word he said—except when their girlfriends were around. Not to mention those girlfriends, who wanted him either in their crosshairs or in their beds.

To ice the three-layer cake of this particular bash, he was going to come face to face with that frigid prig Lacey Clark. Of all the people in the world with whom he didn't want to spend an evening, including Barry Manilow and the guy who'd thought up those stupid Chihuahua commercials, she was number one on his list. After all, it was partially her fault half the world's population—the female half—was out for his blood. She was the one who had given him the reputation of being a male chauvinist without even having to mention his name.

Earlier at the party, he'd seen one pinched-looking, severely dressed woman who might qualify as the schoolmarm he suspected Lacey Clark to be. She was tall and skinny, wearing a mannish black suit, with graying hair pulled into a severe bun. He'd asked Raul, a casual friend and co-worker, to confirm she was his nemesis.

Raul had grinned and slapped Nathan on the back. "How on earth do you do it? I mean, how can you come into a room, look at someone and immediately know who she is?"

"You mean I'm right?" Nate had asked, somewhat deflated to think this woman was indeed the one he was going to share the spotlight with later in the evening.

Raul had shrugged and lifted his hands in defeat. "What can I say? You really are a master of deductive reasoning. I think I'll go on over and say hello to Lacey now. Don't worry, I won't let on to her that you picked her out so easily."

Then the junior editor from *Men's World* had sauntered away, leaving Nate to speculate about the sour-faced crone who'd made his life a living hell for months. He hadn't been able to remain in the same room with her for ten more minutes before he'd made good his escape. He'd meet her soon enough, when the two of them were lucky enough to be congratulated for helping to invigorate the magazines they worked for.

"Here's to you, Lacey Clark," he muttered as he sat in the lounge chair by the pool. "Maybe you'll get lucky tonight, meet some poor SOB with bad eyesight, get laid and get the hell off my back." If anyone sorely needed to get laid, it was Lacey Clark.

As he lifted the bottle of beer to his mouth, Nate noticed the door at the far end of the gym opening in the semidarkness. Hoping he wasn't about to be discovered, he slid lower in his lounge chair, willing the intruder to leave.

No such luck. The person—he could see from here it was a she—slipped into the gym and pushed the door shut behind her. She leaned against it, her body almost sagging. He imagined her sighing in relief, probably glad to have escaped the party. That was at least one thing they had in common. Then she stepped away from the door, into the light cast by an overhead fixture near the rowing machine.

"Man, oh man," he whispered.

She was blond perfection. A teenage boy's breathing, moving erotic dream. From the sleek golden hair falling in a wave past her shoulders to the pale throat, the soft shoulders revealed by the tight black dress and on down the centerfold curves, she was one-hundred-percent pure female temptation.

Nate suddenly found it difficult to pull another chlorine-tinged breath into his lungs. Any words he might have uttered got trapped on his tongue as he watched her toss her small handbag to the floor and bend over to tug her high-heeled shoes off her feet. Well, she couldn't exactly *bend* in her tight dress, she could only lean. When she did, the shimmery fabric pulled taut across her hips and the curve of her rear. Nate shifted in his chair. As she lifted one leg and placed her foot on a weight bench to unfasten the shoe, her dress slid higher, displaying an endless length of black-stocking-clad thigh.

"I think I musta fallen into the pool and drowned, and now I'm in heaven," he managed to whisper.

When she walked to the trampoline, then pulled herself up onto it, he knew damn well that's exactly what had happened.

LACEY COULD HAVE walked down and sat in one of the lounge chairs by the dark waters of the pool, she supposed. But for some reason, the big round trampoline beckoned her. She'd figured no one would be in the gymnasium. If any curious or amorous guests were wandering around J.T.'s mansion, they'd more likely take refuge in one of the richly appointed bedrooms. She had this big, quiet space to herself. All she wanted was to take a moment, to strategize, to figure out how she was going to go back into the office Monday and face her co-workers knowing they'd all feel betrayed after J.T. made his big announcement tonight.

Of course, they were the absolute least of her worries. "I'm sorry, Mom," she whispered. "I'm so sorry. We'll figure out how to handle this."

She wondered what J.T. would think if he could see her now, but couldn't muster up the energy to care. Bracing her palms on the padded mat covering the springs, she pulled herself up and twisted her body around to sit on the metal edge of the trampoline. Careful not to snag her dress, which had set her back a week's salary, she slid backward onto the bouncy surface.

She giggled softly, liking the sense of freedom. Lowering herself, she stretched out until she lay completely on her back. She stared at the ceiling, again grinning at the fit J.T. would likely have if he walked into the room and caught her, in her fancy cocktail dress, lying on the trampoline.

If his latest wife, Deirdre, were with him, she'd probably faint. It already galled the woman no end that Lacey was one of the guests of honor tonight. In Deirdre's social circle, one simply didn't flaunt one's *mistakes* in public.

On that point, she and Lacey were in complete agreement. But she still would have paid money to see the woman's face if she happened to wander by.

The thought made her snicker, and she sat up. Carefully tugging her tight dress higher, she rose to her feet and tested the trampoline with one little bounce. She'd done gymnastics as a kid, and she itched to see if she could still do some of the tricks she'd perfected.

"Not in this dress," she mused. Still, she tugged it higher, knowing no one could see the black ribbon covering the elastic of her thigh-high stockings. No one was around to note the lace of her panties or be shocked that they were the thong type, which left no lines in tight clothes.

Now she was really getting into Deirdre-dropping-over-in-a-dead-faint territory. Thigh highs and a thong? On sensible Lacey, she who preached true love before marriage and emotional commitments before physical ones?

Okay, she had a thing for sexy lingerie. "Sue me," she muttered. So naughty underwear gave her a dangerous thrill. Big deal. She was the only one who ever saw what she wore under her suits and dresses. At the rate she was going in the romance department, that didn't seem likely to change anytime soon!

Lacey suddenly remembered the blond man at the bar and wondered who he was. He'd affected her, distracted her on what was proving to be a pretty lousy night. It had been a long time since Lacey had looked at a man and felt...hot. Needy. And very curious. The wickedly provocative picture that flashed into her mind *really* would have given those who knew her a shock.

Rebelliously, she tugged her dress higher. Not that she lifted it all the way over her hips or anything. But as her feet moved and she bounced up and down, the dress slid up inch by inch until she could feel the cool air of the gym wisping against the lower curve of her buttocks.

It felt naughty, wicked, free and outrageous. And Lacey Clark loved every uninhibited bounce.

Her dress was certainly too tight to try any flips or maneuvers. So she jumped higher, and higher, spinning and twirling in the air, not caring when her hair tumbled riotously around her face and the sweat she'd worried about during the party dripped down her chin. Who cared? It felt good to be bad. And oh, thankfully, she was no longer bored, though she was completely alone.

Or so she thought, until she heard the yell, followed by the splash.

2

IT WAS the thong panties that sent Nate's chair tipping over into the pool. He was no voyeur, but, damn, a gorgeous blonde jumping on a trampoline flashing him a sweet glimpse of her curvy backside with every bounce? What red-blooded American man would be able to resist *that*? He sure hadn't. So he'd leaned just a little too far and gone for an unexpected swim.

The chilly water shocked him. If it hadn't been for the chair hitting him in the head, he would likely have leaped right back out. But the plastic arm of the lounger caught him in the temple, and for a moment or two, he experienced severe disorientation. All he knew was he was in the pool, and a chair and a padded cushion, growing heavier by the second as it soaked up water, were blocking him from the air above.

Before he could move to save himself, someone was yanking him by the arm, pulling him from under the obstacle. When he broke through the surface, Nate sucked in a deep, greedy breath. His rescuer threw an arm across his shoulders and towed him, on his back, to the side of the pool.

When they reached the side, he flung his arm over the pool's edge, as did she. She finally stopped panting long enough to look him in the face.

The blonde. The gorgeous blonde with the peekaboo panties was treading water opposite him. She'd leaped into the pool to save him, not even stopping to consider her dress, which clung to her skin like shiny black Saran wrap. She was an absolute mess. Her sopping hair drooped against her head, sending rivulets of water running down her temples. Her smeared makeup had left black streaks under her eyes. She looked like a wet raccoon. A gorgeous wet raccoon.

Finally noticing his stare, her eyes widened, flashing with something. Confusion? Recognition? He didn't know, couldn't place it, but he saw something change in her expression. She looked out of sorts, confused, perhaps even a little excited. Not surprising given what had just happened. But Nate had a feeling there was more to it than that.

Finally she asked, "Are you okay?"

In spite of the pounding in his head, Nate responded flirtatiously. "I think I might need mouth to mouth."

She frowned. "You're talking. I suspect you're breathing."

He puffed out his cheeks, holding his breath.

She rolled her eyes. "Lame."

"Okay. I give up. I'm fine, thanks to you. I was getting disoriented under the water."

He glanced over his shoulder at the chair, which still floated nearby. As he watched, the cloth-covered cushion sank, disappearing beneath the surface, probably due to the weight of the water. It descended until it rested on the bottom of the pool—right where he might have ended up, had the blow to his head been much harder.

Good grief, he could have drowned! The thought sobered him, sending any flirtatious thoughts out of his mind. "You really might have saved my life. Thank you very much."

He stared into her eyes, which were a fine pale blue that picked up the light reflected on the shimmering surface of the water. Her lips were parted, her breath coming in audible gasps, much like his as they both recovered from the adrenaline rush of his accident.

Close up, she was every bit as enticing, though perhaps in a different way, than she'd been from a distance. Her features were softer, sweeter than he'd expected, given her killer figure. Her heart-shaped face was creamy smooth, and beneath the smeared makeup he could see the tiniest freckles dotting her nose. She looked younger than he'd thought. Definitely not as put together, calm and cool as she'd appeared when she entered the room. Yet the innocent blue eyes and freckles definitely suited the sprite who'd climbed onto the trampoline.

She stared back, looking as though she recognized him. Nate nearly muttered a curse. He waited, wondering if she'd prove to be fan or foe, if she'd coo that she'd read all his articles or tell him to grow up and get a real job.

She did neither. Instead, she sighed, again seeming to be disappointed for some reason, and said, "I didn't see you struggling under the water so I thought you were unconscious."

"The chair hit me in the head."

When she immediately lifted a hand to check his brow, he said, "I'm fine. It just took me a minute to get my bearings."

She pushed his hair back, and the touch of her hand made most logical thought disappear from his brain. Her gesture was gentle, concerned, but the feel of her skin on his felt loaded with additional sensation.

"A minute's a long time to figure out you're underwater." She drew her hand away, looking at her fingers in confusion, as if she, too, had felt something unusual where flesh had met flesh.

"You're right. Maybe it wasn't a full minute," he replied softly.

"It was more like twenty seconds."

"Okay. But twenty seconds too long. I was starting to see my life flash before my eyes."

She raised a skeptical brow. "Really?"

"Well, no, not really, but I did have the sudden thought that I need to call my mother."

"Your mother?"

"To thank her for putting me in swimming lessons, and to wish her a happy birthday."

"You didn't swim," she told him.

"I would have. Ten more seconds, tops. Maybe fifteen. Probably. But I still owe you my life. Thanks again."

She started chuckling. "Do you always talk so fast?"

"Always. In my family, if you don't talk fast, you never get a word in edgewise."

"Is it really your mom's birthday today?"

"No. It's Monday. But while I was under there, I realized if I drowned three days before her birthday, that'd probably ruin the occasion and she'd never forgive me."

This time she laughed out loud. "You do realize this isn't exactly a typical conversation to be having while treading water, fully dressed, in someone else's swimming pool," she said, her eyes alight with amusement.

"Better than the party."

"Yes, I saw you there earlier," she admitted, staring at him intently. "Why on earth did you come here?"

"To hide out," he said, greatly relieved that when

she'd recognized him a few minutes ago, it had been from the party and not from his work at *Men's World*. If she didn't know him, didn't know his name, maybe she would talk to him like the man he really was, not the man he appeared to be in print.

She hadn't said anything, so he continued. "I couldn't take another minute of jovial conversation with people who'd stab me in the back in a second to climb up one more rung of the publishing ladder."

She nodded slowly, obviously understanding, possibly even agreeing. "Okay, I can buy that one. So you were just sitting here by the pool and you accidentally tipped your chair in?" Her eyes widened. "Oh, great, you were watching me, right? That's what happened. You were playing Mr. Peeping Tom and you tipped yourself right into the pool where you could have drowned. All to get a glimpse of a woman's underwear."

"Well, come on, you gotta admit, that is some pretty *fine* underwear."

Her eyes narrowed. "I suppose you're an underwear expert?"

"No, not really." He grinned. "Frankly, I prefer boxers to thongs. I've always thought thongs would be terribly uncomfortable. But you look like you do okay in yours, so maybe I'll try them sometime."

Nate almost regretted baiting her, but she had certainly provided the opening. Now, would she haul herself out of the pool and stalk away in a huff? Or did she have a real sense of humor to go with the killer curves?

Then he saw it. A heartbreakingly gorgeous grin curled her lips, her eyes sparkled, and she chuckled. He heard his own sigh of relief.

Beautiful. Sense of humor. And she'd saved his life. Could things get any better?

LACEY DIDN'T LIKE flirtatious men. Okay, well, that wasn't quite true. She liked Raul, and heaven knew he loved to flirt. But Raul was different. As strange as it seemed, given his reputation with women, she considered him safe. Because he was her brother's age...and her best friend.

This man, however, was far from safe. Gorgeous, sexy strangers with dimpled smiles who flirted and made her heart leap and her thighs quiver were definitely *not* safe.

She'd been shocked when she realized he was the man who'd caught her attention at the party. Within a few minutes she'd realized Raul had been messing with her—this guy was no bonehead. He was sexy, charming and gorgeous. She should have run for cover as soon as he made the mouth-to-mouth comment. Because that had put all kinds of interesting images in her mind!

Instead she continued to hold onto the side of the pool, wearing her sodden dress, which would probably never be free of the scent of chlorine, grinning at the mental picture of him in a thong. "I know of a site online that sells men's thongs."

"And you would know this because..."

"Because I bought a pair for a friend as a gag gift last year."

He raised an eyebrow. "A friend?"

"A female friend who was getting married. She tells me if it hadn't been for the yellow duck on the front, she might have been able to talk her husband into wearing them during their honeymoon."

"I'm with him on that one."

"I suppose you'd prefer your basic black."

"It works so well for you. I'll follow your example."

Lacey should have felt like sinking beneath the water at the realization that this man really had been sitting here watching her on the trampoline. But she laughed again instead. "So do you make a habit out of sneaking peeks at strange women's underwear?"

"You don't seem strange. At least no stranger than anyone else at tonight's gala," he said earnestly. "Do you make a habit out of breaking into other people's gyms during parties?"

"I was hiding out, like you," she admitted. "I hate cocktail parties."

"Me, too. Smiles on the lips, never in the eyes. Superficial conversations. Everybody on the make trying to find someone to hook up with who they won't have to bump into at work the next week."

He sounded sincere, which surprised Lacey. "That's exactly how I feel."

"I'd much rather be treading water in a soaking tuxedo."

"Which is hopefully not rented."

"It is."

"I don't think you're going to get your deposit back."

"Maybe I'll buy it. This might prove to be my lucky suit." Though his tone remained flirtatious, his eyes held a note of serious intensity.

He had beautiful eyes. Green with circles of gold at the center that Lacey somehow felt she could get lost in. They were rimmed by thick black lashes that were unfairly long for a man. And his mouth—that gorgeous, smiling mouth she'd fantasized about after seeing him across the room at the party—was every bit as intriguing close up.

Lacey almost wished she were a different type of person. The type of person who could lean forward and kiss a sexy stranger, because if she didn't find out what his lips tasted like soon, she was going to lose her mind.

She wasn't that type of person, however. She was responsible and conservative, restrained and professional. Any lapses with trampolines, thong panties or to-die-for strangers with amazing lips were genetic flukes, not the real her.

Were they?

"I guess we ought to get out and dry off," she said, hearing a note of regret in her voice. "I imagine I've already been missed. I don't exactly know how I'm going to get out of this one."

"Can't you just slip out, go home without saying anything?" He pulled himself out of the pool, then turned to lend her a hand, easily hoisting her up to stand in front of him on the pool deck.

Before she could reply, she watched as he dropped his gaze to her bare shoulders, no longer covered by the straps of her dress, which had loosened and fallen down her arms. She breathed deeply. His eyes followed the movement of her skin, studying her throat, then moved down to the curves of her breasts. Her heart picked up its pace, beating wildly inside her as this man touched every inch of her body with nothing but his heavy-lidded stare.

She knew she looked a hideous mess. She also knew he wanted her. Not having had much experience with men, Lacey couldn't really say how she could be so certain. Perhaps it was the furrow in his brow, the way his chest moved as his breaths deepened. The way his tightly coiled body radiated heat and energy so powerful she almost felt it snapping across the scant inches separating them.

But he never touched her.

Finally, Lacey pulled her thoughts together, ordered her pulse to stop racing and took a quick step away from him. He shook his head, as if trying to clear his mind, and she knew he'd been as affected as she by the charged moment.

"No, I can't just leave," she said, finally answering his question. "It's complicated." She didn't want complicated right now. For the past several minutes, since she'd leaped into the pool after a stranger, she'd felt uncomplicated pleasure. Sharing laughter and heated glances with a gorgeous man was much better than worrying about J.T.'s plans for the evening.

His plans certainly weren't going to go over very well if she showed up wearing a soaking wet cocktail dress. How could he officially introduce her to Baltimore society and the magazine executives when she looked like a drowned rat?

"I think I'm going to need to call a friend for help."

"I should do the same thing. Do you happen to have a cell phone? Mine's a little wet." He reached into his pocket, pulling out a phone and a small tape recorder, both of which dripped water.

"There's a phone over there by the door," she said. "There's also a bathroom on the other side of the trampoline. You call first. I'm going to try to do something about the way I look."

"You're beyond beautiful," he said with a wistful smile. "Thanks again for saving my life." He accompanied the comment with a tender brush of his fingers against her brow as he tucked her hair behind her ear. Nothing else. Just a gentle touch, and she thought her legs were going to shake apart, sending her back into the water.

"You're welcome." She finally managed to whisper the words on a slowly exhaled breath.

When he turned away and walked toward the phone, she took a few seconds to collect herself. What was it about the man that so intrigued her? His looks were divine, of course, but there was more than that. Perhaps at the party it had been the self-assurance, the appearance of a man totally comfortable in his own skin, that had attracted her attention. A man who could fit in anywhere, knew where he belonged in his world. Unlike Lacey, who was never quite sure where she was supposed to be in life. But now, after their strange meeting in the pool, it was more than fascination. She found herself wanting to talk to him, to hear his deep voice, to see those lips curl up into a smile meant only for her.

Somehow, Lacey found the strength to get her legs moving again, and she headed straight for the bathroom, leaving him to use the phone in privacy. She definitely needed a minute alone to regain her composure.

When she shut the bathroom door behind her, flipped on the light and saw herself in the mirror, she let out a yelp of dismay. Her wet hair stuck to her scalp like a swim cap. Her makeup was mostly gone, and what was left had shifted around so her mascara was on her cheeks and her lipstick on her chin. One of her pretty gold earrings was missing, and if she wasn't mistaken, that was a streak of black dye from her dress staining one shoulder.

Beyond beautiful, he'd called her. Beyond repair was more like it.

AFTER his stunning rescuer disappeared into the bathroom, Nate spent about thirty seconds wishing he'd gone ahead and kissed her the way he'd been dying to as they stood by the pool. If there had been only attraction between them, he might have done it. But there had been more than attraction.

He was seriously interested in her. Interested and intrigued, charmed and amused, and he didn't even know her name! He intended to remedy that, but not right away. He still wasn't ready for the introduction stage. If she was at a party at J.T.'s house, then she probably knew the name Nate Logan. He didn't want any preconceptions to interfere with what might prove to be the start of something special.

Ridiculous, really, to think in those terms about a woman he didn't know. But there had been something magical about her from the moment she'd entered the room. It wasn't just her underwear, though that, of course, had been very special, too. He couldn't put his finger on what so intrigued him about her. The pale blue eyes shining with an innate sense of humor? The light dusting of freckles on her nose, which probably drove her crazy but made him want to lean over to kiss every single one? He didn't know yet, but he planned to find out.

He reached for the phone, then dialed Raul's cell phone number. When the other man answered, Nate could hear the voices and tinkling glasses in the background, meaning Raul was still at the party. He gave him a slightly abridged version of what had happened, not mentioning his blond rescuer. Or the trampoline. And especially not the black thong panties.

"You mean, you tripped and fell into the pool and now you're hiding out in the gym in a soaking wet tuxedo?"

Nate tried not to take offense at the laughter in the other man's voice. "Would you please spread the word that I was called away on an emergency and I'll try to get back in an hour? I should have enough time to get out of here, race home, change and come back. Okay?"

After Raul agreed, Nate hung up and waited for the woman to come out of the bathroom. He tugged off the hated bow tie, which was nearly choking him now that it was tight and wet, and dropped it and his jacket on the floor. Then he kicked off his ruined shoes and socks. When she still hadn't emerged, he muttered, "To hell with it," and started to yank off his white dress shirt. She chose to come out just as he'd pulled the shirt off his shoulders.

The look in her eyes made him glad he worked out.

She froze in the open doorway, her mouth opening slowly but no sound coming out. Her hand rose to her neck, her index finger resting on the sexy spot right in the hollow of her throat. The same spot he'd fantasized about kissing minutes earlier by the pool.

She wore a white terry-cloth bathrobe, and her face was clean, washed free of makeup. The damp golden hair was combed in a sleek wave to brush her shoulders. He couldn't resist looking down the rest of her, at the slim legs and delicate bare feet revealed by the robe. She'd been gorgeous in the black dress. Now, wearing absolutely nothing but the robe—he somehow imagined she'd shed the minuscule underclothes, which had to have been soaking wet—she was deadly.

When he finally lifted his gaze to her face, he noticed
her attention still fixed somewhere around his collarbone. She couldn't seem to tear her eyes off his chest, at
least until he dropped the shirt entirely. Then she
moved her stare to his shoulders. She did absolutely
nothing but look, and he reacted as if they'd shared a
passionate embrace. The woman's covetous eyes had
brought about a strong reaction below his waist. Very
strong. Very pressing.

And probably very damn obvious.

"Uh, you can have..." she stuttered.

A hot amazing night with you?

"That is," she continued awkwardly, "feel free to
take..."

You home with me?

"The bathroom. It's all yours," she finally said as she
stepped into the gym and turned her back to him.

"Sure," he muttered. "And I'm finished with the
phone."

He somehow refrained from touching her as he
walked past her into the bathroom. He shut the door
behind him and leaned against it, wondering how the
sight of her, a woman he'd known for less than an
hour, could reduce him to one large walking case of
need. Those eyes, that smile, those pretty feet and del-
icately boned ankles—she had aroused him more than
any other woman had in his lifetime.

When he'd regained control of himself, he stripped
off the rest of his wet clothes and toweled off. The
towel he'd grabbed from a rack was damp, and as he
used it, he caught a scent of something sweet and flowery, like the smell of his mother's roses that grew on a
trellis along the back porch of his parents' home in
West Virginia.

Her perfume. Her scent filled his head, and he lifted the towel to his face to breathe it in. Suddenly realizing what he was doing, he dropped the towel and glanced into the mirror. Had the blow to his head made him utterly delusional? When he saw the trickle of blood dripping from his hairline, he thought maybe it had.

Hanging in a bathroom closet were several of those white terry-cloth robes, like the one she wore. He grabbed one and threw it on to cover his naked body, then opened the door. "Uh, do you think there's a medicine cabinet or something around here?"

She stood right outside the door, obviously finished with her phone call. "Yes, there is, in the linen closet. Why?"

"I think I need to bandage this."

When she saw the blood dripping down his face, she gasped and ordered him into the bathroom. "Sit!" she said, pushing him toward a vanity stool.

"I can take care of it, if you could help me find the bandages."

"Good grief, why didn't you tell me? Looks like the chair hit you right above the temple and broke the skin."

"I didn't realize it was bleeding."

She stepped closer, leaning down to push his hair back and look at his scalp. He closed his eyes as she nudged his legs apart with her own and moved to stand between them. When she leaned closer, so close he could see a tiny freckle on the top curve of one creamy breast, he couldn't contain a groan.

"Am I hurting you?"

You're killing me!

"Not a bit."

"Can I touch it? I promise to be gentle."

Touch it? Lady, just shoot me and put me out of my misery.

"I trust you." He bit the words out.

She took a wet facecloth and brushed it over his cut.

"Ow," he said with a wince.

"Baby," she teased. "It's tiny."

"It hurts."

"Big tough man." She looked down, obviously to make sure he was kidding and she hadn't really hurt him.

Nate couldn't resist. "I think a kiss would make it better."

"Sorry, I'm not kissing your bloody head."

"I'll settle for a kiss somewhere else," he said with a chuckle.

"Somewhere else? Okay. Constitution Hall," she said dryly. "Five years from Sunday."

"It's a date."

Nate waited patiently while she carefully cleaned his cut, then covered it with some ointment. Every brush of her fingers heightened his awareness. Every time she moved, his senses roared to life. Her scent filled his brain. He memorized the shape of her neck, the curve of her collarbone.

While she helped him, they talked about the party, about the publishing industry, about silly things like thong underwear and swimming with clothes on. He adored the sound of her laughter and used every bit of willpower he had to resist pulling her onto his lap to thoroughly kiss her smiling lips.

At one point, she leaned over and grabbed a small pair of scissors out of the medicine chest on the counter, not noticing, perhaps, that her robe slipped off one shoulder. Nate's heart rate kicked up. He took a deep breath, wanting to reach out and touch her skin with the tip of his index finger. Only that. Just to see if she felt as soft as she looked.

When she turned her attention to him, she obviously saw his interest. She flushed, her face turning a charming pink. Then she casually tugged the robe up and cinched the belt tighter.

"So, you never told me why you felt the need to hide out from J.T.'s party," Nate said, trying to break the heavy, charged silence in the bathroom.

She shrugged. "I guess I felt the same way you did. Superficial people. All ambitious. All on the prowl."

She fell silent, and Nate noticed her hand shaking as she bandaged his cut with some gauze and medical tape. "You okay?"

"I'm wondering how long I can be gone without attracting attention. My friend is going to go to my apartment to get me something else to wear. I can't just disappear."

"Right. It's complicated," he said, remembering her earlier comment.

"Exactly."

"Complicated for you? Or for someone else?"

She stepped away from him, from between his legs, and busied herself putting away the medical supplies. "Several someone elses, as a matter of fact," she admitted.

Nate heard a quiver in her voice and noticed her eyes were shiny and bright. "Hey, are you okay? I didn't mean to upset you."

"You didn't. It's not you. It's tonight, this party." She paused. "J.T."

Nate snorted. "You know the old reprobate personally, do you?"

She paused, her eyes widening with surprise. "You know him too?"

Nate shrugged. "As much as I want to. Has he been bothering you? Is that what's going on?"

A rueful smile spread across her face. "He's bothered me. Not in the way you think." Then she shook her head and turned to put away the medicine kit. She took her time about it, peering intently at something on the shelf of the linen closet with her back to him. Nate saw her take something off the shelf and slip it into the oversize pocket of her robe before she closed the closet door.

When she turned, her eyes were bright and sparkling. She bit the corner of her lip, suddenly looking both mischievous and nervous. Nate considered asking her if she'd just stolen something from J.T. Birmingham's bathroom, wondering if the superrich used some exotic type of toothpaste, but she distracted him by pointing to his robe.

"So is someone bringing you some clothes?"

"No," Nate admitted as he stood and followed her out of the bathroom. Some of the forced intimacy caused by their close proximity in the bathroom evaporated in the cavernous gym area. "I planned to run home to my apartment to change. Unfortunately, while I was undressing I realized my keys are no longer in the pocket of my wet pants. I imagine they're somewhere at the bottom of the pool, meaning I take another swim or I come up with another way to get some clothes."

"Could you get someone to go by your place and pick something up for you?"

"Yeah, I probably could. My neighbor keeps a spare key for me, so I could call and ask him to let someone

in," he replied. "In the meantime, I guess we both hide
out here." He walked to the trampoline and leaned
against its edge. "So have you got all the jumping out
of your system?"

"I think so."

"It looked like fun," he said, trying to tempt her.

"Help yourself," she said. "I promise not to peek at
your underwear."

He contemplated telling her he wasn't wearing any,
but didn't think it wise.

"So, why do you dislike J.T.?" she asked as she
walked over and sat on the bench of a weight-lifting
machine.

Since there was nowhere else to sit unless they
moved to the pool area, Nate went ahead and hopped
onto the edge of the trampoline, sitting on the padded
springs. "I don't dislike him. He's a heck of a business-
man. But I see him for what he is."

"That being?"

"I don't know. What do you call a man in his sixties
whose new fourth wife is less than half his age? Plus he
still manages to hit on any attractive single woman he
meets." Nate sighed in disgust. "My sister came in to
the office to visit last month. She was holding her one-
year-old baby, and J.T. still flirted with her nonstop."

"Some women find him charming."

He snorted. "Maybe his bank account. Believe me, if
I had his money, there are plenty of things I'd do with
it other than invest it in future alimony payments."

"Like?"

"I dunno. Feed the hungry? Help inner-city moms
pay for day care?"

"How politically correct," she said, her dry tone displaying her skepticism.

He took no offense. She didn't know him, after all. Why should she believe he had any interest in social issues? "Okay, then I guess I'd buy a private island."

She grinned, stood and walked over to stand beside the trampoline. "Can I join you?"

"On my island?" He gave her a playful smile and gestured to the black fabric surface. "Please do."

He held out a hand to help her climb up. Forcing himself to look away, he deliberately tried not to notice when her robe gapped open again, displaying several long inches of pale, smooth thigh.

"And what would you do on this island?" she asked.

He slid back, pulling her with him until they both sat on the surface of the trampoline. Stretching out to lie on his back, he put his hands behind his head and looked at the ceiling. "I'd ban cocktail parties."

"Good start," she conceded as she stretched out to lie beside him. "What else would you ban in your kingdom?"

"Bow ties. Tuxedos."

"I think tuxedos are very sexy," she murmured.

Nate glanced over to find her staring innocently at the ceiling, as if she hadn't just said something blatantly flirtatious. Or perhaps she hadn't. Maybe he'd misread her.

He hoped not.

"Can you ban control-top panty hose, too? And size-one cover models who make the rest of us look fat?"

"You got it. And self-help books. No Mars and Venus crap allowed in the libraries on my island."

"You don't care for relationship books?"

He turned to look at her, waiting until she met his eye to answer. "The right couple involved in the right relationship has no need for books. When it's there, when it's real, you know it. And if it isn't, no book is going to make it work."

She held his stare, her eyes wide, glittering in the low lighting of the room. "Is it there for you? Have you found your perfect partner?"

Nate was unable to resist the slow smile that curled across his lips. He reached over, tucking a nearly dry blond curl behind her ear. "Ask me tomorrow," he whispered.

Her eyes widened as she caught his meaning.

He knew it was crazy, given their brief relationship, but something was happening between them. They were in sync. They spoke with the same rhythm, laughed with the same sense of natural joy...looked at each other with the same sense of intrigue.

It was more than physical, more than titillating or exciting, more than a delightful interlude.

"Something's happening here, isn't it? Something amazing." He didn't move toward her, letting his words and his voice be the only indicators of the depth of his interest in her. The next move was hers.

She made it. When her eyes narrowed slightly, zoning in on his mouth, he knew she wanted to kiss him. She leaned closer, tentatively, and he didn't move, knowing somehow that she had to do this, had to be the initiator.

Then, with a soft sigh, she brushed her lips against his. Focusing all his thoughts on the sensation, he remained still, letting himself be kissed by this woman whose name he didn't yet know. Letting her move closer, move over him, cup one side of his face with her soft, cool palm.

She tilted her head, parted her lips slightly. When her tongue slid out tentatively to taste him, Nate's restraint began to skid away. He groaned and finally moved his arms to pull her on top of him.

The kiss deepened. Emboldened by his response, she increased the tempo, driving him crazy with each caress, each stroke of her sweet, wet tongue. He met her every move, anticipated and joined her when she turned her head for deeper access. Somehow, some way, she slid off him, falling to her back on the bouncy surface of the trampoline, pulling him over her. Or perhaps he pushed her. He didn't know. Thought was gone, replaced entirely by sensation.

Nate waited for the voice in his head to tell him to stop, to insist it was insane to be making out with a woman he'd known an hour. But he couldn't think, couldn't focus on anything but the way she tasted— like sweet, intoxicating wine. The way she smelled—of roses and springtime. The way she made him feel—on fire and nearly out of control.

The gentle give-and-take of their bodies moving together on the springy surface filled his mind with images of making love to her. Right here. Right now. While a party continued in another part of the house, while his boss looked for him and his tuxedo lay wet on the bathroom floor. All he wanted was to toss away their robes and roll over her, onto her, *into* her, on this little fabric island. To see if this sense of rightness between them extended to the physical as well as the emotional.

It would. He knew it would. Knew it the way he knew the roads leading to his family home, the way he knew the right words to use in a story, the way he knew his own nature.

This beautiful blond stranger with the laughing eyes

and the smiling lips could be the person he'd waited for all his life. He *knew*.

"Can something like this really happen?" she asked when he moved his mouth from hers to press kiss after kiss on her jaw, her earlobe, the long column of her throat. Her voice held longing. Desire. Wonder.

"It can," he whispered as he moved lower to kiss her shoulder. "It is."

Then he couldn't think, couldn't focus on anything except the feel of her body, smooth, pale and ripe beneath the terry-cloth robe. He inhaled her sweet flowery scent, knowing it had imprinted itself on his brain and he'd never be able to sit in a rose garden without thinking of her for as long as he lived.

A little hitch of a moan emerged from the back of her throat when he slipped his hand under the robe to find the curve of her breast. She arched into him, offering herself, crying out her pleasure as he teased her pebbled flesh with his fingers.

Somehow their robes slipped open until they hung from their shoulders. Not shrugged off, but covering nothing. Skin met skin. The hair on his chest rubbed her pert nipples, seducing him further. Unable to resist, he bent over to nibble gently on the curve of her flesh before taking the taut tip into his mouth. She cried out, buried her hands in his hair and leaned toward him.

Her thighs parted slightly, and Nate groaned as he became aware of a deeper scent, an earthier essence of their combined arousal. His body responded, instinctively driving toward her, pressing against her, silently asking her in an age-old dance of desire, *Will you?*

Her eyes opened lazily, her breath growing choppy

as she slid her legs apart, welcoming him, giving him her answer. *Yes.*

It made no sense. They were strangers. They were in someone else's house. But Nate knew if he didn't take this miraculously sensuous gift he would wonder *what if* for the rest of his life.

As if sensing his thoughts, she said, "I know. We'll wonder later how this happened. Not now. Now I want your hands on me."

Nate was happy to oblige. He ran the flat of his palm down her body from her throat, over the full curves of her breast, down her soft, flat belly. Lower. When he slipped his fingers between her legs he found her slick and wet. She shivered and let out a moan, which Nate echoed. "You're sure?" he asked huskily, giving her one more out, though it nearly killed him to think of not finishing what they'd started.

Instead of answering, she reached into her robe, which lay open beneath her. When she retrieved something from the pocket and held it up to show him, Nate smiled.

"I don't know why I took this when I saw the box in J.T.'s linen closet." She tentatively bit the corner of her lip as the two of them stared at the small packet in her hand. "Is it wicked? Have I shocked you?"

Nate laughed softly, then reached out and plucked the condom from between her fingers. "Not wicked. Delightful."

He lowered his mouth to hers for another long, wet, languorous kiss. When her hands moved down his body in an appreciative, lingering caress, he almost shook with his need to be inside her. Then she moved her hand lower, taking his erection in her hand. Her head fell back and her eyes closed as she explored him with her fingers until Nate had to physically pull away to avoid ending this interlude a hell of a lot sooner than he wanted.

"I want you inside me now, please," she whispered, her eyes still closed, a sultry smile curving her pink lips.

Needing no further invitation, Nate sheathed himself with the condom, then moved between her thighs, taking another moment to taste the warm, moist skin of her neck.

She whimpered and slid one incredibly soft leg around his hips, urging him closer until he was poised at the hot, wet entrance of her body. He'd barely begun to move into her when she thrust her hips up, engulfing him, taking what he'd intended to offer her slowly and gently.

"Yes," she cried, her voice echoing in the huge room as she took him all the way inside her.

Nate had to stop, to suck in a breath. Had to get accustomed to the most intensely pleasurable sensation he'd ever experienced. It went beyond sex, beyond physical. He felt like it was his first time. He'd never imagined that physical sensations could so quickly be enhanced by emotional ones.

"I can't believe..." she began, then paused to gasp as he slowly withdrew from her body, only to plunge again. Deep. Fast. His every movement was enhanced by the bounce of the trampoline, setting a wonderful, unique rhythm to which they both began to dance in earnest.

"I've never...that is, I think I'm going to..." When her cries grew louder and he saw the telltale flush rising in her body, Nate knew she was close to climaxing.

"Yes, do," he whispered against her lips as he

changed his movements, rocking against her until she hissed her delight. She caught his motion, using his lower body to apply pressure to her most sensitive spot. Nate slowed his movements, allowing her to take what she needed, watching her face as she finally reached that peak of pleasure. And only after he saw that moment, heard a fulfilled cry that bordered on a scream, did he follow her to his own soul-shattering release.

Afterward, Nate watched her beautiful face, watched her breaths slow, her color return to normal. Finally, when she opened her eyes and gave him a pleased, languorous smile, he gently pulled out of her and pressed a soft kiss to her lips.

"I need to know your name," she said dreamily. "So I know what to cry out the next time."

"And I need to know yours," he finally said when their lips broke apart again. "So I can know who now owns me body and soul."

She stretched lethargically and kissed his jaw. Lifting a shoulder, she allowed the robe to fall completely off one arm. As he bent lower to taste that sweet, smooth skin, she whispered, "My name's..."

Before she could finish, the door opened and an overhead light flashed on. Nate didn't want to believe it. He wanted to believe it even less when he looked toward the open doorway and saw who stood there.

"J.T." he said. "Oh, boy."

"Oh, boy is right," the woman in his arms echoed, her horror undisguised.

J.T. Birmingham entered the room with Raul directly behind him. Nate couldn't meet his friend's eyes, which had grown as round as saucers as he spied Nate and the gorgeous blonde tangled together—arms, legs

and bathrobes. Wanting to protect her, Nate shifted
slightly so they could see only his terry-cloth-covered
back. She took the moment when she was shielded
from their stares to pull her robe together over her naked, trembling body.

"Son, you're wearing my robe," J.T. finally said, his
voice calm and steady, betraying no hint of his mood.

Yeah, he was caught by a millionaire, wearing the
man's robe during the middle of an important cocktail
party at which he was a guest of honor. Caught having
sex with a gorgeous stranger on that man's trampoline.

"Can things get any worse?" he muttered.

"And," J.T. finally continued, "you're lying on top of
my daughter."

3

LACEY LET OUT a small groan of dismay from beneath the gorgeous man whose touches had thoroughly intoxicated her. This couldn't be happening. None of it.

She hadn't fallen into the arms of a complete stranger whose name she didn't know, had she? She couldn't just have participated in—no, *initiated*—the single most intoxicatingly sensual act of her entire life, could she? She wasn't feeling damned put out at the interruption—rather than embarrassed—because she so wanted to roll on top of this man and make love to him again on their pretend *island,* to use her mouth on every inch of his body and beg him to do the same, was she?

"Yes, yes and yes," she muttered from beneath him.

His body stiffened. "He's really your father?"

"Biologically speaking," she admitted. She didn't elaborate. The story was too long, the hour too late and her nerves too frazzled to go into ancient history now. Especially since they still lay tangled in a passionate embrace while her father and Raul watched from a few feet away.

"You could have said something earlier."

Lacey saw his embarrassment. He was obviously thinking of the comments he'd made about J.T. She certainly hadn't been offended, since she felt pretty much the same way he did about her father's romantic track record.

When she glanced over and saw the speculative look on J.T.'s face, she sighed. He'd been telling her for years that she needed to let loose, to give in to her true nature. He'd insisted she stop hiding who she really was, as her stepfather had forced her to do throughout her childhood.

She didn't imagine this scene was exactly what he'd had in mind when he'd pictured Lacey letting loose. Then she giggled, amused in spite of the awful situation in which she suddenly found herself. *Lacey Lets Loose. Sounds like a porno title.*

"Hi, J.T.," she said. "Uh, can you give us a minute?"

He didn't argue. "One minute." Taking Raul by the elbow, her father led him out of the gym, giving them privacy.

Sliding out from under the man who'd driven her to a wildly intense orgasm just moments before, Lacey tugged the robe tighter and cinched the belt. Her lover stood and offered her a hand up. They walked together to the edge of the trampoline and he gently helped her down, leading her to think he wasn't truly angry she hadn't mentioned her relationship to J.T.

Without a word, he turned and went into the bathroom. She instantly knew he had to get rid of some evidence. Somehow that brought another laugh to her lips, which her father caught when he walked into the room. She saw a twinkle in his eye and knew he was fighting to prevent a grin.

"Having a nice evening, dear?" he asked, his voice still deceptively calm. He turned his attention toward the bathroom door as Lacey's gorgeous stranger emerged to join them next to the trampoline. "And you, too?"

"It's going just swimmingly," her lover muttered.

"Just the word I was going to use," Lacey said. Hearing Raul snort a laugh, she leveled a glare in his direction. "Thanks a lot, Raul."

"It wasn't my fault." Raul held up a hand, palm out. "He followed me."

"You two know each other?" her lover said, looking back and forth between Lacey and Raul.

"Seems everybody knows each other pretty well now." Raul's grin held a note of merriment that instantly put Lacey on guard.

J.T. cleared his throat, demanding their attention. "Anyone want to fill me in on what's going on here? I saw this character skulking away after I asked him if he knew where the two of you were. And I find this." He still sounded calm, but a bright look of interest and amusement remained obvious.

Most fathers would have been anything but amused. J.T., however, wasn't like most. He was probably overjoyed that straitlaced Lacey, the illegitimate child he hadn't even laid eyes on until she was twelve years old, apparently had some of her real father's blood running through her veins, after all. Exactly as her stepfather, the man she'd *thought* was her real father for the first several years of her life, had feared.

"This man fell in the pool," she explained, knowing she sounded ridiculous. "He hit his head. I had to help him out."

"And what? He needed mouth-to-mouth?" Raul said with an evil chuckle.

She glared.

"Can someone tell me why you and Mr. Logan were

here, anyway, when you're supposed to be guests of honor at my party?" J.T. asked.

"I needed some air," Lacey replied. "I would have been back in a few minutes, no one would have missed me. I'm sorry I..."

She paused. Thought about what J.T. had said. Staring hard at Raul, she whispered, "Logan?"

Her friend shrugged and gave her a look of complete innocence—which was completely feigned.

"Well, Nate, what's your excuse?" J.T. asked, apparently oblivious to the fact that Lacey's blood pressure had risen to the point where she thought her head was going to blow off.

Nate? Nate Logan? "Please, no, anything but that," she said to Raul, her tone insisting he put her fears to rest.

He just smiled.

"I'm sorry, J.T., similar story to, uh, your *daughter's*. I needed some air, came down here to sit by the pool for a while and fell in. She really did leap in to save me, so I'm completely at fault for her missing the party."

Lacey didn't care to be defended by her archenemy. If he really was her archenemy. Could he be? Could this wonderfully witty, charming stranger be the man she'd so disliked in print for so many months? How could that be possible when he'd made her feel the way no one had ever made her feel before in her life? Like she could lose herself in him. Give herself body and soul to him. Explore every sensual possibility between man and woman yet still be safe and cherished in his arms.

Could he *really* be Nate Logan, famous for coining the phrase, "So many bimbos, so little time"?

"This is a nightmare," Lacey said as she turned and

walked away from the three men, pressing her hands against her heated cheeks. She kept her robe tugged tightly around her body and moved to stand beside the pool. As she stared at the shimmering surface of the water, looking for answers that weren't to be found, Lacey felt herself growing less embarrassed and more angry.

First of all, she was going to *kill* Raul. He'd known all along who the man was by the bar. If he'd told her, she would never have found herself in this position. She might have pulled Nate Logan from the pool, but once she'd recognized whom she'd saved, she certainly wouldn't have bandaged him. Much less *really* bounced with him on that trampoline!

The memory brought heat to her cheeks. How could she have wanted him so much? How could a single hour in the company of a handsome man have her forgetting who she was, what she believed? So much for her protestations about true love, monogamy and emotional commitment. A sweet-talking, hunky guy with a chest she wanted to eat off of had gotten her flat on her back faster than any of her previous dates had held her hand!

The question remained. Why hadn't Raul told her? Why had someone she thought was a good friend kept silent? Yes, Raul had a wicked sense of humor, liked to play jokes. Maybe he thought the evening would be more interesting—for him—if Lacey had no idea the man she'd been so attracted to was her nemesis.

"You jerk," she muttered, knowing it was probably the case.

Obviously not getting the hint that she wanted to be alone, the three men came closer. Lacey heard their voices as they moved to stand beside her by the pool and nearly threw her hands into the air in frustration.

"Well, I suppose I can make excuses. After all, it's not every day I find my daughter in a compromising position. Honey, I was beginning to worry about you. Now I can tell you're a perfectly normal, healthy young woman." J.T.'s hearty chuckle made her wince.

Oh, wasn't that just peachy. Her father was thrilled to find her making out with a stranger. He'd probably offer them a bedroom next. Her stepfather, of course, would have been reaching for his shotgun.

"I am going home." Lacey bit the words out.

"Like that?" Nate gestured toward her robe.

Lifting her head in haughty dismissal, she turned her attention to her father. "Could you please see if Deirdre has something I could borrow to wear out of here?"

"If you two kids want to, uh, wait here, Raul and I will find something for you both to wear. Might take a while."

She heard the suggestiveness in her father's voice and shot him a vicious glare. "I'll wait upstairs, then. Alone."

Her father shook his head. "Now, Lacey, it'll be awkward enough to hold off making the announcement tonight. You really think I want to have to explain why you're dashing around my house half naked, too?"

Before she could reply, Lacey heard a choking, coughlike sound and glanced over her shoulder.

Nate Logan was bent over at the waist, hacking into his fist. Raul, whose laughter could be heard even over Nate's coughing, whacked the other man in the back.

"Are you all right, son?" J.T. asked, looking concerned.

Nate ignored him. When he'd finally regained his breath, he said, "Lacey. Not Lacey Clark." He stared at her intently, shaking his head as if to order her to say no.

Finally beginning to see this whole situation from his point of view, Lacey remained silent. Obviously he hadn't known who he was making love with any more than she had, nor did he like it any better. She slowly nodded.

His eyes widened in shock, and his mouth dropped open in disbelief. "You're Lacey Clark?" he finally managed to say. "*You're* the frigid virgin femi-Nazi?"

Any sympathy Lacey might have felt for the man at having been as embarrassed as she was by the situation evaporated. She reacted instinctively. And for the second time that evening, Nate Logan found himself taking an unexpected swim.

LACEY DROVE HOME in the robe. After she'd shoved Nate the Nitwit into the pool, she'd turned on her heels, grabbed her purse and shoes and exited the gym. She hadn't watched as her father and Raul helped Nate out of the pool. Nor had her stride broken when Nate had bellowed, "You'll pay for that!" as she walked out of the gym, slamming the door behind her.

Though sorely tempted to exit through the middle of the party, Lacey had slipped out a kitchen door and found her car on the darkened lawn. Her drive home had been quick and furious, matching her mood, and she knew it was a lucky thing she hadn't been pulled over. *Good evening, officer, my license and registration? Yes, sure, let me check the pocket of my robe!*

All she wanted to do was escape but the next morning, Saturday, she sat on the small balcony of her apartment, sipping a cup of tea, and wondered what had happened after she left. The phone had rung once during the night, but she'd spied the caller ID box and ignored it. She hadn't forgiven Raul and was in no mood to talk to him.

When the buzzer sounded from her front door, she wondered for a second if he'd come over to grovel—or to gloat—in person.

"Lacey, I know you're home. I need some chocolate!"

Grinning as she recognized the voice of her friend and neighbor, Lacey answered the door. "Good morning, Venus. Why, exactly, do you need chocolate at eight a.m.?"

Venus Messina, who lived one unit over in the three-story building, breezed into the apartment looking a wreck. Her bright red hair wasn't in its usual big and fluffy style. Instead it was lying flat and lank against her head. Her makeup was smeared off, and she wore a black leather minidress and fishnets. Even looking a mess, however, the woman was striking. Six feet tall, curvy and buxom, with a look in her eyes that dared anyone to mess with her, Venus was everything Lacey had ever fantasized about being as a kid. Tough, fiery and hard as nails. Right down to her last Irish-Italian bone. Everything Lacey was not.

"All-nighter?" Lacey asked as Venus beelined for the kitchen.

Her friend didn't acknowledge the question. "Don't hold out on me, sugar. You know what I need."

"There's Godiva on the bottom shelf, behind the yogurt."

Venus gave a coo of pleasure as she found Lacey's stash of expensive chocolate and helped herself to a few sizable chunks. "Mmm, with enough chocolate I can almost forget that I just got dumped."

"Oh, V, I'm sorry," Lacey said. She didn't ask who the dumper was, since Venus changed boyfriends every few weeks. Almost as often as she changed hair color. "You okay?"

"Things were great," Venus said as she grabbed more chocolate and followed Lacey into the living room. "We clubbed all night, went to his place, had a romantic breakfast. Then he tells me he's getting back together with his college girlfriend and this was our last night together."

Lacey scooted over on the sofa, making room for Venus to plop down next to her.

"Of course, since it was only our third night together, I shouldn't feel this bad, should I?" Venus stuffed another piece of chocolate into her mouth, leaned her head back and shut her eyes. "Men are such dogs."

Lacey sipped her tea. "I won't argue there."

Venus must have heard something in her voice. She opened one eye and glanced at Lacey suspiciously. "What happened?"

Lacey shrugged.

"Oh, my gosh, last night was the party! The big night. I'm sorry, doll, I forgot all about it. You okay? Have you talked to your mom yet?"

Lacey sighed, knowing the phone would probably be ringing any minute. Her mother had been in a panic when they'd spoken the night before. Lacey hadn't been able to muster the emotional energy to call her yet. "J.T. didn't make his big announcement."

Venus looked surprised. "I thought you said he was committed to going through with it."

"He was. Something, uh, happened to interfere with his plans." Lacey curled her legs, tucking her bare feet under a cushion of the sofa. "I guess that's one positive result of what has to be one of the worst evenings of my life."

"Well, what on earth happened? Your father's been chomping at the bit for a year to announce to the city of Baltimore that you're really his daughter."

Venus was one of only a small group of people who knew the truth of Lacey's parentage. A group that had increased by one last night when Nate Logan found out. She cringed. "I had a little accident and ended up ruining my dress during the party."

Venus snorted. "So, you took my advice and did the old dump-a-bloody-Mary-on-your-lap routine to make your getaway."

"Not exactly." Lacey began to explain to her friend what had taken place the evening before. She tried to avoid some parts—mainly the makeout session on the trampoline, the unexpected intensity of passion between her and the man she hated, the whole sex-with-a-nameless-stranger thing.

Venus didn't buy it. "So your father walked in and found you and some guy wearing bathrobes in the gym. So what? It's not like you were..."

Lacey flushed.

"Whoa-ho, you *were!* You were doin' the hootchie cootchie dance with a hunka man you fished out of a swimming pool."

Lacey knew her silence spoke volumes.

"Was he good?"

"Venus..."

"Oh, come on," Venus said with an impatient shrug. "Forget that you're hating yourself this morning and thinking you're a trampoline tramp. Did the man rock your world last night or not?"

Lacey couldn't lie. "Rocked it big time. Cripes, Venus, I didn't know it was *possible* for an orgasm to be strong enough to blow off the top of my skull. I shook for five minutes!"

The redhead let out a shriek of laughter. "Girl, I *knew* you could let loose if you tried."

"Why is everyone so altogether concerned about me letting loose? My father probably would've offered to let us have his whole house for the night if I'd expressed the least bit of interest. Do you know how bizarre that is?" Lacey muttered as she stood and went into the kitchen to make more tea.

Venus, the first friend Lacey had made when she moved to Baltimore to make it on her own three years before, followed, giving Lacey an awkward pat on the shoulder. She looked almost remorseful for her words, which wasn't a typical expression. Venus typically had a screw-you look on her face, one suited perfectly to her attitude.

Her attitude had something to do with her upbringing, Lacey imagined. And their upbringings couldn't have been more dissimilar. Lacey had been raised under the rigid, watchful eye of her stepfather, a former Army sergeant turned minister, and her mother, a Betty Crocker, June Cleaver wannabe who'd had one tiny lapse of judgment in her otherwise proper youth. The misjudgment that had resulted in Lacey's birth twenty-six years before.

Venus had grown up in the child welfare system in south Jersey, scratching her way through high school and out of the foster home where she'd been raised. The only thing they had in common was their complete confusion during their childhood about who their fathers were. At least Lacey had eventually found out. That's more than she could say for Venus.

"Everyone wants you to be happy, honey," Venus said, "including your real dad. I think he sounds kinda cool."

"In a Hugh Hefner way, I suppose," Lacey retorted. "My mother sure went from one extreme to another, didn't she?" Lacey started. "My mother! I guess I should call her."

"I know you're worried about what's going to happen to your mom if everyone in your hometown finds out you were illegitimate. But it's the new millennium. Does anyone really care about that stuff anymore?" Venus asked.

"Maybe not here. Maybe not in New York or L.A. But in Smeltsville, Indiana?" Lacey gave a bitter laugh as she steeped another cup of tea, then added lemon and sugar. "Yes. People care. People would care that the wife of the respected Reverend Clark of the Smeltsville Methodist Church had given him an illegitimate child as a present when he got back from serving his country in the military."

Venus nodded miserably. They'd had this conversation before. "I know, Lace. Of course you're right. I'm sorry your father doesn't understand."

"Believe it or not, my father doesn't want my mother hurt. He has some feelings for her still." Lacey hadn't believed that at first, but the look on J.T.'s face when he talked about the whirlwind romance he'd had with her mother all those years ago made her think he was sincere. "The thing is, he felt cheated out of the first twelve years of my life. He has no other children. And he wants the world to know I'm his."

"Can't really blame him."

"No, I can't. If it were just my mother and stepfather, maybe we could find a way to make this turn out all right."

"Your grandparents, right?"

Lacey nodded, feeling tears gather in the corners of her eyes. "This could kill them, Venus. Finding out their only granddaughter *isn't* their biological grandchild at all? That their daughter-in-law cheated on their son and he accepted her illegitimate baby? How can I let it happen?"

The truth was, she couldn't. In the years she'd been in Baltimore, her father had given in to her pleas to remain quiet. It was only recently, with the phenomenal success of Lacey's column in the magazine, that her proud, strutting father had started pushing her to let the world know who she really was.

He'd warned her months ago that he was going to do it. When she'd realized she couldn't dissuade him, Lacey had started trying to work things out with her mother, hoping she'd find the strength to deal with the scandal if the word got back to someone in Smeltsville, Indiana. And it would. J.T. Birmingham was a well-known millionaire playboy and world-renowned publisher. The word *would* get back.

"Well, I guess you lucked out last night," Venus said as she dug another piece of chocolate out of Lacey's fridge. She broke it in half, handing the bigger piece to Lacey. "Maybe something else will happen to make him change his mind."

"It was a reprieve." Lacey nibbled on the chocolate. "A delay, not a solution. I still have no idea what I'm going to do to convince him not to go through with it."

For a moment, Lacey thought Venus was going to

forget to question her about her romantic interlude. She should have known better. Venus would never forget anything that had to do with Lacey's rather Spartan love life. She'd been telling her for months it was time for her to find a man.

"Okay, sweetie, time's up," Venus said as she licked the last of the chocolate off her fingers. She took a carton of milk out of Lacey's fridge and took a couple of mouthfuls straight from it. Lacey rolled her eyes.

"We've wallowed. We've gorged. Now...talk!"

NATE LOGAN wasn't too surprised to find a message from J.T. Birmingham on his desk when he arrived Monday morning. "Now comes the firing," he mused as he crumpled the pink notepaper in his hand and two-pointed it into the trash can.

He really didn't know if he was going to be fired over Friday night's serious lapse in judgment. J.T. hadn't seemed exactly outraged. And if any firing were to be done, he imagined it would have taken place in the heat of the moment. Still, the man had had the entire weekend to think it over...and perhaps to be influenced by his little girl.

Nate didn't know which was worse. That he'd had out-of-control sex with his boss's daughter or that the daughter had turned out to be Lacey Clark. In any case, he was about to find out what Friday night's debacle would cost him, as J.T. wanted him downstairs in his office on the tenth floor in half an hour.

The entire twelve-story downtown Baltimore office building was owned by J.T. Birmingham's company. The *Men's World* offices were on the twelfth floor, and the *For Her Eyes Only* staff worked on the fifth. That was one reason he and Lacey Clark had never bumped into each other. There were, after all, a few thousand people working in the building daily. And Nate did a lot of his work at home on his computer, telecommuting and usually only coming into the office one or two days a week. He'd come in today, of course, to see if an ax was going to sink into the back of his neck.

"I've got a meeting," he told Raul as the other man entered his office. "And I'm not talking to you, anyway."

"Oh, come on, how was I supposed to know you and Lacey had gotten so...friendly? I mean, I've never even heard her mention holding hands with a guy, much less falling to the nearest flat surface with one ten minutes after meeting him."

Nate paused, pointing an index finger toward Raul in warning. "Watch what you say, Raul."

Raul's eyes widened. "Are you defending the honor of your sworn enemy to *me*, one of her best friends?"

Nate swiped a hand through his hair, not liking the amused tone in Raul's voice. "Stay out of it. It's between me and Lacey." No, things weren't finished between he and the thong-wearing blonde. She might like to imagine her shove into the pool was the last word on the subject of their relationship, but she was wrong. They had a *lot* to talk about. Starting with how a beautiful, passionate and responsive woman like Lacey could write the drivel she dished out in her column!

Raul interrupted his musings. "And J.T."

"Which is who I'm going to see right now. Why have I never heard he had a daughter? I mean, why isn't it the scuttlebutt around this place?"

Raul glanced toward the partially open office door

and lowered his voice. "Very few people know, Nate, and that's how Lacey wants it."

"The rich girl didn't want the world to know Daddy got her her cushy job?"

Raul's disapproving frown told him what he thought of that. "J.T. had no idea Lacey was even working for the magazine until after she climbed her way up through the ranks into the writing staff. She did it on her own. We met when we both started here—me as a mail carrier, her as a clerk."

"But why? If she wanted a writing job—hell, if she wanted her own column—wouldn't Daddy have just given it to her?"

"She didn't want it that way. And if you don't know why then you obviously don't know her very well yet."

Better than you can imagine, pal.

"Please, Nate, it means a lot to Lacey. It's been hell for her, trying to protect her mother and her family when J.T. has been dying to announce to the world that she's really his daughter. Don't say anything in front of anyone else, please?"

Nate wondered at Raul's loyalty. For a smart-ass college dropout who'd made his way up through the publishing house with his biting, sarcastic wit and sharp editorial eye, Raul suddenly sounded awfully mother hennish.

"Gotta go. It wouldn't do to be late for my own execution," Nate said with a shrug. "Don't worry. I won't say anything," he added before he left the room, noting Raul's nod of relief.

Ten minutes later, Nate was sitting in a waiting area outside J.T. Birmingham's office. He'd had just enough time to open the copy of *For Her Eyes Only* he'd picked up off a coffee table before the door opened and J.T. bellowed, "Is Nate Logan here yet?" The man poked his head out, saw Nate in the waiting room and beckoned him in.

He looked like he had a smile on his face. *Do rich men smile when they're about to fire someone? Possibly.*

Nate followed him into the office and saw two people already there. One was his boss, the editorial director of *Men's World*, Chuck Stern. The other was a woman he knew from the staff of *For Her Eyes Only*.

Maybe J.T. was into public executions.

"Good morning, everyone," he said as he took the seat toward which J.T. had pointed.

The others nodded. Chuck immediately turned his attention to the big boss. "Great party Friday night, J.T.," he said with an overly enthusiastic nod.

Nate sunk lower in his chair. He did not want to talk about Friday night...especially not in front of witnesses!

The woman editor—Maureen, he remembered—was not to be out-brown-nosed. "Oh, yes, your wife was so charming."

You should meet the daughter.

Before Nate could say anything, the office door opened again, and in came the very person he'd been thinking about.

"Hello, Lacey," J.T. said as he stood and ushered her to the last empty chair in the office.

Nate took a minute to study her, looking for the sprite from the trampoline, the humorous pool rescuer, the woman who'd felt like heaven in his arms. They were obviously hiding today. This Lacey Clark was all business—buttoned up, hair pulled back, dressed in a navy suit and white blouse. At least the skirt was short.

From where he sat, Nate was able to appreciate the length of those gorgeous legs.

The memory of the way they'd felt wrapped around his hips soon had him shifting in his seat.

"Well, we're all here," J.T. said.

Lacey finally glanced around the room toward the others. She nodded at Chuck, smiled at the woman, then her eyes met Nate's. He couldn't resist a wink.

"Oh, great," he heard her mutter from a few feet away.

"Chuck, Maureen and I have spent some time this morning discussing a new project," J.T. began.

"It was all J.T.'s idea," Chuck interrupted.

"A brilliant one," Maureen said.

Nate leaned back in his chair just far enough to catch the slight rolling of Lacey's eyes.

J.T. ignored the blatant sucking up. "We've decided to do a first-ever crossover feature between *Men's World* and *For Her Eyes Only*."

Crossover feature? Nate didn't like the sound of that.

"It's quite obvious to all of us that your two columns have sparked a great deal of interest in our magazines, which was why we were going to thank each of you with these bonus checks Friday night." J.T. held up two envelopes, but didn't go into any more details about Friday night. "It seems a flirtatious battle of the sexes is raging across the country, thanks to your columns. We get a combined thousand letters a week about them."

Nate wondered which of them got more, percentage wise, of that thousand. He thought it prudent not to ask. Lacey glanced at him out of the corner of her eye. When their gazes met, he saw her eyes narrow and knew she was thinking exactly the same thing. The knowledge brought a chuckle to his lips. So, Ms. Clark had a competitive spirit, did she?

"The point is, we've decided it's time for the two of you to go head to head. Work side by side. Hand in hand."

If he said in and out, Nate was going to lose it.

"Please knock off the metaphors and get to the point, J.T.," Lacey urged. Nate noticed the shocked glance Lacey got from Maureen, her boss. Obviously the other woman did not know about Lacey and J.T.'s relationship.

J.T. chuckled fondly. "I'm getting there, Lacey." It seemed incredibly obvious to Nate, now that he knew what to look for, that J.T. looked on his daughter with affectionate approval.

"What we want is for you and Nate to work together, to prove, once and for all, which of you really has their finger on the pulse of American romance today. Lacey, you prove to Nate, and to the world, that the perfect man really is the sensitive storybook hero you write about."

Nate snorted.

"And Nate, you go out and show Lacey why you're so sure purely physical relationships are the *only* ones men need."

"I don't quite understand...." Lacey began.

"Well, to put it simply, you two are going undercover. From now on you and Nate Logan think together, work together, write together. You're a duo on a covert mission."

Nate watched the blood drain out of Lacey's face and felt his jaw tense.

J.T. continued as if he hadn't noticed his daughter's sudden, obvious horror. "Lacey Clark and Nate Logan are now officially partners on the battlefields of the sexual revolution."

4

LACEY WAITED until Chuck and Maureen left J.T.'s office before she made her position clear. Her father had obviously seen the fire in her eyes, because he'd asked the editors to excuse them while he, Lacey and Nate worked out the details. Once the others were gone, Lacey stood and leaned over J.T.'s desk. "No way. There is no way I'm doing this."

"For once we agree about something," Nate murmured from his chair in the corner of the office.

She ignored him. "J.T., the two of us are oil and water."

"Looked more like oil and dipstick to me," J.T. mumbled. Lacey immediately cursed herself for providing him the opening. She glanced over her shoulder, praying Nate hadn't heard. He was looking at the ceiling, all wide-eyed innocence, a tiny grin playing about those much-too-kissable lips. He'd heard, the bastard. "That's not funny."

"Lighten up," her father said. "Put yourself in my position, why don't you? I've got the two hottest writers in the country working for my magazines. Your print war has done more to boost circulation than any special feature or advertising campaign we've ever launched."

"So why don't we keep up what we've been doing? I'm quite sure each of us has lots more to say without having to work together," Lacey said, almost desperate.

"The timing's right. It's the perfect setup. You're both professionals, so just resign yourselves and make this work."

Lacey heard J.T.'s seldom used I-will-brook-no-nonsense tone, the one he'd used on her the time she'd run away from home and made her way to his mansion in Baltimore as a teenager. Of course, that time his *first* reaction had been pure joy that she'd finally taken a stand against her conservative stepfather. Frustrated and defiant, she'd fled from her Indiana home as fast as her self-righteous fifteen-year-old legs could carry her. If she remembered correctly, that particular incident had been over a boy, a school dance and a red dress. J.T. had eventually sent her back, despite her pleas and her fit-throwing anger, using the same tone he was using now. She sighed in resignation.

"What do we get out of this?" Nate asked, his voice deceptively light. She'd almost forgotten he was there. Leave it to him to get right down to dollars and cents.

"Another bonus." J.T. held up the envelopes on his desk. "One that'll make this one look like a kid's bubblegum money."

Nate shrugged. Lacey watched him, wondering why an avaricious glint didn't immediately glow in those deceptive, gorgeous green eyes.

It had been awful sitting in the meeting with him. She'd forced herself to focus on J.T., trying not to glance over, not to let a blush stain her cheeks as memories of their interlude on the trampoline hit her again and again. She'd been able to think of little else all weekend. Though she'd refused to answer Raul's calls or to go into too many details with Venus, there was simply no way to erase Nate Logan from her mind. A memory couldn't be turned off like a phone or avoided like an intrusive question.

He'd charmed her. Intrigued her. Made her laugh. Made her burn. Made her mad as hell. Aroused her more than she'd ever been aroused in her entire life. And made love to her like something out of a seductive fantasy.

Lacey could still feel every touch, remember the weight of his body on hers and the incredible sense of tight fullness she'd experienced when he'd been buried deep inside her. Shuddering, she forced the mental image away, clamping her thighs together as her thoughts inspired her body to betray her.

J.T. noticed Nate's seeming disinterest in the financial side of his offer. "Well?"

Nate rose from his chair, unfolding his tall, lean body slowly, radiating the self-confidence that was such a part of him. Not wearing a tux today, he was almost more devastating dressed casually in jeans and a dark green shirt. Maybe not quite as devastating as he'd been in the robe the other night. Or beneath that robe. Oh, the man's body was the stuff orgasmic dreams were made of!

"Finances aren't always the bottom line," Nate finally said, his tone still calm, his voice still quiet.

Lacey snorted and nodded toward her father. "Don't try telling him that."

"What else is it you want?" J.T. leaned back in his chair, crossing his arms in front of his barrel chest. Lacey saw the sparkle of anticipation in his eyes. He'd moved right into his negotiator pose. Her father loved to make deals. She'd learned by the end of her first two-week visit to his home at age thirteen never to play Monopoly with him.

Nate crossed the office and stood by the window, looking out as if he had all the time in the world. "Nice view."

Lacey bit the corner of her lip to hide a laugh as her father cocked his head and tapped his fingers on his desk. J.T. oozed anxious impatience. She had to admit, Nate was handling him very well. Better than she had.

J.T. raised a brow. "You want my office?"

"Nah," Nate said, turning to flash a devastating grin over his shoulder. The curve of his lips reminded her of his kisses, the way he'd licked the sensitive white skin below her nipples before closing his mouth over her. The sensation of his tongue on her breasts had sent spirals of heat through her body to pool between her legs. She felt it again, just remembering. Lacey had to grab the back of a chair to steady herself.

"This view would be too distracting for writing," Nate continued. Though she knew he was talking about the outside view, he was staring right at her, an appreciative expression on his face, as he said it. She held the chair tighter.

"A raise? A trip to the company condo in Saint Croix?" J.T. asked. "What?"

Nate met her eye. "Company condo? Sounds interesting. But not really for me. I'm more of a ski vacation person."

J.T. blew out an impatient breath.

"So what is it you do want?" Lacey finally asked, unable to contain her curiosity. *Dancing girls? A subscription to the hootchie of the month club? Me staked out naked near a fire ant nest, covered with honey?*

His grin widened, and he gave her a tiny, flirtatious wink.

Another numbingly erotic mental image intruded. *Me staked out naked covered with honey...in your bed?*

"You know, writing columns is a good gig," Nate finally said. "But it's not exactly *feature* writing...."

Lacey understood where he was headed. A grudging smile of respect crossed her lips. "Now he gets to the point."

J.T. leaned back in his chair. "I'm not sure we need another feature writer. There are several members of the staff with a lot more years on the team."

Nate shrugged and smiled. "Sure. And hey, you know, I'm sure any one of them would probably be a better match with Lacey for this crossover piece."

Lacey watched her father's eyes narrow as he realized Nate was prepared to walk away from this assignment. Then he nodded. "You pull this off, and I imagine we could find some room for another feature writer." He pointed an index finger toward Nate. "As long as you're willing to keep up with your columns."

Nate agreed. "I can write the columns in a week. I've got the rest of the month to sink my teeth into some real projects."

"I do like your attitude, son," J.T. said, the compliment both rare and sincere.

"And I do like your view." Nate again turned to look at the blue, cloudless summer sky.

Lacey watched the two of them, so alike in their self-confidence, yet so different in appearance and method. Her father used bluster and an over-the-top, outrageous style to get what he wanted. Nate used charm—the boyish grin, a soft voice, those twinkling green eyes—to achieve his ends.

They were both just as happy as pigs in mud.

"Uh, I hate to be the spoilsport in this whole love fest," she said, "but I haven't signed on for this. He gets what he wants. That doesn't mean I'll go along."

Surprisingly, it wasn't her father who answered. Nate turned, leaning his hip casually against the edge of her father's desk. "You're right, Lacey. Obviously it won't be much of an event if the two key players in this war aren't both in agreement. Isn't there *something* you have to gain out of it? Something you want that would make it worth having to put up with working with me for a month or so?"

Nate stared at her. A smile of encouragement and a small nod told her he had something particular in mind. And suddenly she knew what it was.

"I think I'll leave you two to sort out the details," Nate said, obviously noticing her sudden comprehension. "J.T., thanks for the opportunity."

He turned to leave. Lacey had to wonder how he'd known, how he could have realized there *was* something she wanted from J.T. Somehow, he knew she wanted to keep her relationship with J.T. quiet. She'd find out how later. For now, it was her turn to negotiate with her father.

"Lacey, if you can work things out, why don't you stop by my office when you're finished here and we can, uh, talk."

She heard the tiny hesitation in his voice and knew it was intentional. Talk? Sure, they'd talk. And this time, that was *all* they would do.

THERE WAS NO QUESTION in Nate's mind that Lacey would come to his office when she'd finished meeting with her father. If she was the type of woman she appeared to be, he imagined she'd be barreling in here any minute, ready to lay down the law, to take charge, to set the boundaries for their assignment.

It was lucky for him he knew she *wasn't* the woman she appeared to be. The Lacey Clark of the printed page—the Lacey Clark who'd been all buttoned up, argumentative and stiff-backed in her father's office—could never replace the Lacey Clark who'd leaped after him into the pool. Who'd climbed up onto the trampoline. Who'd worn those thong panties.

"Right on cue," he muttered when his office door was forcefully pushed open. An unsmiling Lacey Clark walked purposefully into the room and sat down in the empty chair across from his desk. He thought it prudent not to mention that he'd just been thinking of her, and her underclothes.

"You're really going to go through with this?" she asked, getting right to the point.

"Yep. And you? Did you work everything out with J.T.?"

She gave a curt nod. "I've agreed. We have just under four weeks to research and write our stories. Yours will appear in the October issue of *For Her Eyes Only*, mine in the October issue of *Men's World*. Here's what I think we should do first."

He held a hand up, palm out, stopping her. "I think what we should do first is talk about Friday night."

"No. What we should do first is *forget* Friday night ever happened and get to work."

"How can I forget that you saved my life?" Nate asked with a tender grin. "And you bandaged me up?"

She cast a quick glance toward his temple, and Nate turned his head to show her the small, healing wound.

"You've recovered. Forget it."

Lordy, she was stubborn. He liked that in a woman. "Am I supposed to forget everything else about Friday night, too?"

She just stared.

"If I forget, then I can't very well apologize, can I?"

Her stiff shoulders loosened slightly under her silky white blouse. "You...you want to apologize?"

He nodded, doing his best to look sincere. "I am *so* sorry, Lacey, so terribly sorry I forgot to lock the door of the gym."

It took a few seconds for his meaning to sink in. Then her eyes widened in shock. He waited for it. Which would it be? The shriek of outrage? Or the wicked grin he knew damn well was lurking behind her beautiful pink lips?

Before he could tell, she covered her mouth with her hand. Standing, she turned her back and walked toward his heavily laden bookshelf. Finally, she squared her shoulders, turned to face him and said, "You've got a big mouth, Logan. It's going to be a real pleasure showing you up in the October issue."

"Keep dreaming," Nate retorted with a grin. "By October, when those magazines hit the stands, you'll be admitting your white-knight romance superhero is either fictional or gay."

She threw her hands into the air and muttered something toward the ceiling.

"Have a habit of talking to yourself?"

She caught his eye and leveled a haughty stare in his direction. "I was praying for restraint."

"Please don't restrain yourself on my account. I think I like the unrestrained Lacey I met Friday night."

"Friday night I didn't know the person I rescued was a sexist jerk."

"You always believe everything you read? Don't you ever trust your own instincts?" Nate asked, bothered that she refused to look beyond his magazine work to the real man. Some people saw only what they wanted to see. He hated to think Lacey Clark was one of them, since the moment they'd met Friday night, he'd found her captivating. She seemed so different in person than she was in print, much like himself.

Maybe this assignment wasn't such a bad thing. It would force them to work closely together, to get to know each other, if she let it. Which was still questionable, since she appeared to have all her defenses up.

"I have excellent instincts," she retorted.

"Sometimes. Your instinct Friday night was to trust me, to live for the moment, to go along for the ride of something pretty spectacular. Today your instinct is to hate my guts."

"Today I know who you are."

Nate rose from his desk, walked around it and approached her. She took a tiny, nearly imperceptible step back. He saw her pulse beating wildly in her throat. Though she maintained a nonchalant pose, she was not at all calm. "No, Lacey, you don't. You don't know me any more than I know the real you."

She stared at him, her eyes shifting lower to look at his mouth, and he knew she was thinking of their kisses. He sucked in a deep breath, remembering the feel of her in his arms, the way her scent filled his head, the way her body felt deep inside. Like heaven on earth. Like ecstasy. Like home.

"Can't we wipe the slate clean for now? Start off this assignment with open minds, each willing to explore the possibilities?" he asked, keeping his voice low and soothing. "We both have something to gain out of this."

She shifted from foot to foot, nervous, anxious, reacting to their closeness almost as much as he was.

"Your feature-writing job," she finally said.

"And you get to keep your secret a little longer."

She pulled her rapt attention off his mouth and looked into his eyes. "How did you know about that, anyway?"

"Raul said it wasn't common knowledge. He didn't say why."

She shrugged, sidestepped and took a seat in the chair again. "It's a long story."

"Family, right?"

"Yes, family," she said softly. "I do appreciate you not saying anything to anyone."

"I, for one, applaud a family who knows how to keep secrets." He shook his head in disgust. "Mine definitely does not!"

"Oh?"

"There's not a single topic that isn't discussed ad nauseum around the Logan family dinner table on holidays. Right down to what color underwear my mother bought my father last Christmas or whether my twenty-year-old brother got lucky with the head of the cheerleading squad after the homecoming game."

She nibbled a corner of her lip. "Did he?"

Nate lifted his hands, palms up, and chuckled. "What can I say? He's his brother's brother."

"Sounds like your family's very close."

He nodded. "Thankfully, most of them live a few states away so I still have a few moments of privacy each year. And as the target of their matchmaking, advice and never-ending opinions, I have learned the value of keeping my mouth shut."

She responded with a skeptical lifting of one eyebrow.

"I might talk a lot, but I know when to shut up."

"You certainly kept quiet about your name," she muttered.

"As did you. Your timing was impeccable on that one."

"Touché," she admitted with a tiny, grudging smile.

"So, J.T. agreed not to out you if you did this assignment?" he finally asked when she didn't continue. He didn't mind changing the subject. He had a feeling if they started talking about Friday again, she'd clam up or leave. Which would be a damn shame since, for the first time today, they were finally talking with the same sense of easy interest they'd shared the other night.

She nodded. "He gave me until the end of the year, which will hopefully be enough time for my mother to work things out."

"I have to admit it's strange to me," he said as he moved closer to lean his hip against one corner of his heavily laden desk. He nudged a pile of papers and folders out of the way and scooted back until he sat on the desk's edge, just above her. "Your father is one of the richest men in the country, and you don't seem too eager for anyone to know about it."

Lacey tried not to be distracted by the lean male body mere inches from hers. He was so at ease, as always, so comfortable and laid-back. How could he be laid-back when she was so tense? How could he appear so unaffected when three minutes ago she'd been desperate to yank him to her and kiss him senseless?

How could he sit there, looking so gorgeous, when he was a despicable jerk? "Um, what?"

He grinned. "You okay?"

"I'm fine," she insisted between gritted teeth.

"I guess I still have a reporter's instincts. I smell a good story here and I'm curious."

His comment broke the aura of sensuality in which Lacey had been sitting. She clenched her fingers around the armrests of the chair and sat up straighter. "There is no story here. This is not for public consumption. I have six more months and I need every one of them. So stay out of it. You and I have an assignment. It's purely business."

He again held up a hand, palm out. She noticed his hands were not pale and white, like many of the other guys who worked in an office nine to five. His were tanned, roughened, and she had a sudden memory of the feel of them on her body. Her heart skipped a beat.

"Hey, no problem. Strictly business."

She breathed a sigh of relief.

"We've got our assignment. We need to work together to do the job we're being paid to do," he continued. "And if you can forget all about climbing on top of me on that trampoline, then I'm sure I can forget all about those black thong panties."

"I CAN'T STAND Nate Logan," Lacey muttered as she walked into her office late that afternoon after a round of meetings.

She didn't realize the room wasn't empty until Raul spoke. "Sure didn't look that way Friday night." Raul sat in a vacant chair in her office, leaning back with his hands folded over his chest. His crossed feet were on her desk, muddying up a folderful of reader letters Lacey planned to work on later in the week. He'd been nosily reading them, and she caught a smirk on his face as he put one letter on her desk. "Some pretty lovesick people in this world."

"Don't you have your own office?" she asked as she shoved Raul's feet off the desk.

"Tell me about your meeting with J.T. this morning."

"How do you know about the meeting?" Lacey shrugged. "Never mind. You know everything that goes on around here."

"So, are you two going to work together on this story?"

She sighed. "Yes, it appears we are."

Raul laughed out loud and rubbed his hands together. "Perfect. I knew you and Nate would hit it off."

Lacey, who had taken her seat at the desk, put one fist on her hip and cocked an incredulous brow. "Excuse me?"

"Oh, I meant professionally," he said with a sheepish grin. "Really. I know the two of you are so passionate about your jobs you'd be a great writing team."

Lacey remained skeptical. "Right. And that's why you let me think Nate wasn't the guy I spotted at the party Friday night?"

He waved a hand airily as if it didn't matter at all. "I didn't want to spoil the surprise. The buildup between you two has been going on for months. It wouldn't have been fair for you to know who he was before he got to see you, now, would it?"

Well, yeah! "Remember, my friend, paybacks are hell. One day all your misdeeds will come back to haunt you," Lacey said.

"I'm shaking in my shoes."

Since Raul knew how much was at stake in Lacey's personal life, she filled him in on the agreement she'd reached with her father. His sincere happiness for her made it almost possible to forgive him for his rotten trick Friday night.

"It's quitting time. Let's go to happy hour," he said.

Lacey glanced at her watch. "Actually, I already agreed to meet Venus at Flanagan's at five-thirty."

"Ooh, Amazon woman? Even better," Raul said. "When are you going to fix me up with her?"

"She chews up and spits out little boys like you for a snack."

"So let's go."

"Well, sure, Raul," Lacey said as she tidied her desk for the night, "feel free to join us."

Before he could reply, Lacey's desk phone rang. Holding up a hand to silence him, Lacey answered. As soon as she heard her mother's voice, she dropped to her chair and waved Raul out. He blew her a kiss before leaving, whispering that he'd meet her at the Irish pub up the block in a half hour.

Ten minutes later, after a teary, stressful conversation with her mother during which Lacey assured her at least fifteen times that J.T. would keep his word and not reveal their family saga to the press until the end of the year, Lacey hung up and breathed a deep sigh of relief.

"Can't think about your decades-old affair anymore, Mom," she muttered as she cleaned up her desk for the day. "Not when I've fallen smack-dab into a crazy, reckless affair of my own!"

As she prepared to leave, Lacey wondered how she could be so angry and yet so reluctantly amused by Nate Logan with each encounter they shared.

The man was a smart-ass, no doubt about it. He liked saying outrageous things, trying to get a rise out of her. Yet he wasn't always being intentionally goading, she knew. Part of it appeared to be his forthright personality, an attitude of let's cut the crap and get down to the issue at hand, which came across so strongly in his writing.

She supposed she had to be thankful to him for prodding her in J.T.'s office. Of course, she would have eventually realized what she could ask of J.T. in return for doing the assignment. She hadn't needed Nate to think of it first. But he had, and she did appreciate it, deep down.

She hated that. Hated appreciating anything about him. Because there was too much she liked about him already. Correction, too much she *had* liked before learning his name.

"Why couldn't you be Joe Blow, an accountant from Jersey?" she asked out loud. As she flipped off her overhead light, she acknowledged the truth. If he'd been an average Joe Blow from Jersey, she probably wouldn't have found him so devastating Friday night. His self-confidence had attracted her, his flirtatious charm had intrigued her, his embrace had seduced her.

And that self-confidence, charm and embrace had been all pure one-hundred-percent Nathan Logan.

5

FLANAGAN'S PUB was located a few blocks off Charles
Street in an area of office buildings and trendy restaurants. Surrounded by businesses that catered to professionals seeking a good spot for lunch meetings, Flanagan's was one of the last few old-time bars on the
block. The pub's wood floors were pitted and stained,
its booths sticky, its vinyl-covered bench seats torn.
They served lots of beer, lots of whiskey and absolutely
no umbrella drinks. A few nights a week some of the
locals would gather to start up impromptu Irish music
sessions, with fiddles, tin whistles and bodhran drums.
There was no pretense in the building or the servers,
and it was Lacey and Venus's favorite after-hours
hangout. Since Venus's foster uncle Joe owned the
place, they came here quite often.

Waiting for Venus and Raul, Lacey tucked herself
into an empty booth near a front window. Fortunately,
she'd arrived early, because a half hour later, with
happy hour fully under way, there would be no free ta-
bles.

Though it was a work night, Lacey figured she deserved a beer after the day she'd had. She ordered one
from their regular dour-faced waitress. The woman
had just thumped a mug of beer down on the scarred
wooden table and walked away when Lacey noticed a

pair of men's boots, topped by faded blue jeans, standing in the aisle.

"Well, Miss Clark, imagine running into you here."

Not really wanting to, Lacey raised her eyes anyway
and saw Nate Logan standing there. Raul stood behind
him, his grin impossibly wide, a sparkle of excitement
in his big brown eyes.

"You're dead meat, Raul," Lacey muttered.

"Yeah, you are, Raul," Nate said before he slipped
into the booth to sit across from Lacey. He leaned close
so she could hear him over the chatter from nearby ta-
bles. "I didn't know you were going to be here. I
wouldn't have come if I'd known."

That pricked her ego. "Feel free to turn right
around."

Instead of coming back with a retort, Nate held her
stare. "I didn't mean I'm not happy to see you. I meant
I wouldn't have come knowing you didn't want me to.
If you'd like me to go, I will. We have to work together.
We don't have to socialize."

Lacey shrugged. "Well, since we *are* going to have to
work together, we probably should declare a truce."

"I didn't know we were at war."

"Don't you read your own press?"

"Yes, but unlike you, I don't usually believe it. Besides, I thought we declared our truce Friday night."

Lacey frowned. "Bring up Friday night again, and
I'm outta here." From the seat next to her, which Raul
had just taken, she heard annoying squawking noises.
I'm not a chicken!

Nate lifted a hand for the waitress. Lacey watched as
the previously dour woman become a jittery, giggly
bundle of femininity while Nate ordered his beer.

"It's not his fault," Raul said, leaning over to whisper in her ear. "This happens all the time. I think it's the dimples."

Good grief, if he had women fawning all over him all the time it was no wonder the man had an ego the size of the Key Bridge! Though, actually, when she thought about it, Lacey had to admit the truth. She'd found him many things Friday night, but egotistical wasn't one of them. Charming, yes. Flirtatious, yes. Hot and gorgeous, yes, dammit. But not arrogant.

"So why are you friends? I wouldn't picture you much enjoying the competition," Lacey said with a smirk.

Raul raised an eyebrow. "No competition. He's Matt Damon to my Ben Affleck."

Lacey snorted. "Keep dreaming."

Nate finally turned his attention toward them as the waitress sauntered away, a little more jiggle in her step than Lacey had noticed before. "What were you saying about dreaming?"

Lacey felt her face flush. "We were talking about movie stars," she muttered, shooting a quelling glance at Raul.

Shrugging, Raul turned his attention to several women at the next table. "Let the flirting begin," Lacey said as her friend spoke with a brunette in a red sundress.

"I had a dream the other night." That drew her attention to the very gorgeous, distracting man seated across from her. She almost kicked Raul to get him to turn around so she wouldn't have to deal with Nate Logan alone. Since the brunette in the sundress was flirting back, however, she figured Raul wouldn't appreciate the interruption.

"About an island," Nate continued.

Lacey's heart skipped a beat as she remembered their playful conversation on their trampoline island. The sparkle in his eye told her that's exactly what he was referring to.

"Oh?" Lacey asked, her voice not much above a whisper.

"A place where dreams become reality. Fantasy Island."

She cleared her throat nervously, then crossed her arms. "Should I start calling you Tattoo?"

He grinned. "No, I'm the owner of the island, remember? No cocktail parties, no size ones, no elevator music."

"You didn't mention the elevator music," she retorted.

"Thought of it later," He gave her a wry grin. "'We Will Rock You' just doesn't work without words."

She chuckled in spite of herself, then immediately clamped her lips together. *Snap out of it. He's a jerk!*

"So you do remember Friday night, after all?"

"One or two things," she admitted as she sipped her beer, wondering how she could feel so languid and hot, so cozy and intimate with him in a room with dozens of other people.

"Yeah. One or two things," he repeated, his eyes growing heavy-lidded as he moved his gaze down her body in a long, deliberate, visual caress.

Despite herself, Lacey felt a sudden, intense reaction. Her nipples grew tight and sensitive against her blouse as her pulse sped up. She sucked in a deep breath and shifted in her seat. He obviously noticed. By the time he met her eye, his flirtatious expression was gone, replaced by heat. Pure heat.

"Anybody ready to do it?"

Lacey gasped and turned to stare in shock at Raul. When he held up an empty beer mug, she realized he'd been asking if they were ready for another drink. Catching Nate's eye, she saw his amusement and nearly groaned.

"I'm ready," Nate replied, his voice smooth and seductive.

"You're always ready," Lacey snapped. "I'm not. One's quite enough for me, I don't plan on going for a second round."

Nate raised an eyebrow. "That a challenge?"

"Not for me."

"I think a gauntlet's been tossed."

Raul stared at them both like they were crazy. "What are you talking about? Do either of you want another beer or not?" When they both declined, Raul turned to the brunette.

"It won't work, you know," Nate said, his voice low.

"What won't?"

"This front. These barriers. I met the *real* you, the Lacey who can laugh and flirt, fantasize and entice."

She gulped. "I don't know what you're talking about."

"Sure you do. I'll be here when you're ready to admit it."

Before Lacey could respond, she heard a shout from the front door. "Waitress, if there's a pint of Guinness on my table before I get to it, I'll leave you a huge tip!"

Venus.

"Ah, Amazon woman," Raul said, immediately turning his attention from the brunette. His eyes narrowed in appreciation as he watched Venus approach.

"Chews up. Spits out," Lacey muttered.

"Back off, Mama Bird, little chick's ready to soar like an eagle," Raul said.

She smirked. "Or get plucked like a hen."

Nate enjoyed listening to the banter between Lacey and Raul. The two of them sounded like bickering siblings, reminding him of his relationship with his sister. When Lacey talked to Raul, he saw glimpses of that same sense of casual friendliness he'd shared so briefly with Lacey Friday night.

Maybe he would have cause to thank Raul later for tricking him into coming along and ambushing her here. For a moment or two, when they'd looked at one another, they'd both been remembering the same flash of attraction that had overwhelmed them at the party. She almost let her prickly, protective wall down. If he could catch her in more moments like that, perhaps they'd have the chance to really get to know one another.

Though she'd probably never believe it, Nate very much wanted to get to know her better. To find the sparkling woman he'd made love to Friday. Then to make love to her again...and again. He also wanted to feel that same sense of rightness he'd felt, a feeling he'd never experienced before, as if he'd finally found his perfect woman. Unfortunately, his perfect woman had ended their magical evening looking at him like he was something she'd scraped off the bottom of her shoe. But he'd find her again. Damned if he wouldn't.

Before Nate realized someone was joining them, a woman plopped herself down on the empty half of his bench seat. Turning in surprise, he found himself nose to nose with a buxom, laughing redhead.

"Who've we got here then?" she said, giving him a frank, appraising once-over. She was as tall as he, though the poofy bright red curls gave her at least an extra inch of height. Her green eyes were full of laughter, and her too-bright lips curled into a huge smile. "Yum, yum," she said with a deep, appreciative sigh. "My name's Venus, darling, and you would be?"

Before Nate could answer, Raul interrupted. "Venus, since when do you drink Guinness?"

"Can't help it. It's the Irish air in here." The redhead shrugged. "Now, back to the question at hand. Who might you be?"

"Nate Logan," Raul supplied as he leaned across the table to try to get the woman's attention. "Now, talk to *me*."

Venus didn't even look at him. "Go 'way, little boy."

Nate had to grin at the woman's frank, overblown approach. "And you are?"

"Venus, lovely man, goddess of love and all that," she said with a moist-lipped smile. Then a frown tugged at her brow. "Oh, dear, did he say Logan?"

Nate nodded. *Here it comes. She's a* Men's World *reader.*

She pursed her lips and gave Nate a long, thorough stare, her eyes lingering on his face, his chest and then his jeans. Finally, she looked up and raised a curious brow. "So, *you're* the trampoline man."

Nate almost choked on his mouthful of beer. Across the table he saw Lacey sink lower into her seat.

"Uh, yes, that would be me," he finally said, unable to suppress a grin as he realized Lacey had been talking about their interlude. When she finally dared to glance his way, he met her stare, silently challenging her to admit she'd been talking about him. Thinking about him. Her cheeks grew pink. Then she nibbled her bottom lip and finally, beautifully, broke into a tiny, helpless grin.

"Geez, you're tactful, Venus." Lacey shook her head ruefully. "Why not get up on the bar and announce it?"

Venus ignored her. She was still blatantly staring at Nate. Finally, she blew out a sigh of resignation. Glancing at Lacey, she said, "Okay, I'll keep my claws off. Heavens, Lacey, when you decide to let loose, you certainly choose the right person to do it with."

Nate glanced again at Lacey and saw her sigh and roll her eyes. Her amusement didn't completely hide her embarrassment.

Lacey Clark might surround herself with unusual, perhaps even outrageous people—Raul, Venus, heck, even her own father. She seemed determined, however, to stick to her mature, responsible self-image. It had to be tough. From the moment he'd first laid eyes on her, Nate had seen glimpses of the irrepressible part she tried to hide. Perhaps her choice of friends was a glimpse into the workings of her mind. She couldn't be true to herself, so she surrounded herself with people who were? Just as her choice of underclothes betrayed her longing to be free of her perfectly respectable outer attire? He didn't know, didn't understand her yet, though he was determined that he would.

Nate enjoyed the next hour. Lacey wasn't quite the free spirit from the trampoline, but neither was she the ball-breaking businesswoman from her father's office earlier that day. For the most part, she sipped her beer, watching with detached amusement as Venus held court and Raul drooled. Her indulgent smiles at her friends told him she wasn't angry with either of them, though Raul had obviously set her up by inviting Nate to come along, and Venus had been downright flirting with Nate since the minute she'd arrived.

Toward him, however, Lacey remained cool and polite. That would have frustrated him to no end had he not seen so much in her face before Venus arrived. Lacey had looked...hungry. Not predatory, not greedy or avaricious. But full of hunger. Full of need.

That was enough to keep him here, though she'd tried to retreat behind an impersonal wall. She couldn't remain entirely aloof, however. Throughout the evening, she kept sneaking glances at him when she thought he wouldn't notice. He felt her eyes on him, felt her confusion and her desire, probably because it mirrored his own. He did his fair share of looking whenever she was distracted.

Of course there eventually came one moment, one heady, intense moment, when their eyes met. They both looked at the same time, saw the same expressions at the same instant. He should have looked away. Or she should have. Neither did.

"Lacey?" he said softly, leaning closer.

She bit her lip, obviously knowing he'd seen the expression in her beautiful blue eyes. He had to admire her courage, though. She leaned in to hear what he had to say. "Yes?"

"Keep looking at me like that and I might forgive you for pushing me in the pool."

As color flooded her face, Lacey turned her head and wouldn't look at him again. Finally, after another half hour of shop talk, the topic eventually turned to their assignment.

"So, Nate, you get to be a sexist jerk in a *woman's* magazine, huh?" Venus said. "Hope you have a bullet-proof vest."

He heard Lacey's snorted laugh and caught her eye. "You think it's going to be so much better for you? How many men are going to be thanking you for filling up the pages of *Men's World* with poetic advice about how they can become white knights?"

"Women don't want white knights," Lacey countered. "They just want real emotional integrity."

"No, what they want is a guy with a fat paycheck and a big package," Raul interjected, looking disgusted.

"And preferably no wife and kiddies waiting at home," Venus added with a nod.

"Whose side are you on?" Lacey asked her, looking disgruntled. "You're telling me the money and the...*equipment* are the two key things you look for in a man?"

Venus took her sweet time thinking about it. Nate had to lift his mug of beer to his lips to prevent a laugh at Lacey's dismay. "Looks like you're in the minority," he murmured.

"I don't think so." Lacey narrowed her eyes at her friend, a look Nate interpreted as *I'll get you later!* Then she said, "I guess we'll find out when we get to work."

"How about we start bright and early tomorrow?" Nate said. "Where's a good place to meet young, unattached Americans interested in the whole relationship thing?"

"Singles club," Venus immediately offered.

Nate spoke. "Laundromat."

"The library." That was Lacey's suggestion.

Raul spoke with more certainty than any of them. "Self-serve car wash."

"A car wash?" Venus crossed her arms and gave him an incredulous look. "You gotta be kidding. What woman wants to meet single guys when she's a sweaty mess from washing her car?"

"One who looks good in a wet T-shirt," Raul replied. "Duh!"

Seeing Raul wince and bend over, Nate knew Venus had just kicked him under the table. Personally, he hadn't thought about it before, but Raul's idea had merit. "So, we check out a library, Laundromat, singles club and a car wash?"

Lacey shook her head. "*We* don't check out anything. You're free to do your own research on your own time."

"Doesn't sound very partnerly. We're in this together, remember? I think that's what old J.T. asked for."

She looked like she wanted to argue, but could only sigh in resignation instead. *Gotcha!* As long as J.T. was giving her what she wanted, Lacey was going to have to play the game by the rules. Meaning they were going to be spending a lot of time together. He could hardly wait.

A few minutes later, Nate glanced at his watch. "Time to hit the road. Thanks for the invite, Raul. It was good to meet you, Venus. Lacey, I'll be seeing you."

Before he could stand to leave, however, Venus moved her arm too quickly and knocked her entire drink into his lap. The redhead immediately leaped up, grabbed a handful of napkins and moved to clean it up.

"Uh, it's okay. I can get it," Nate said, taking the napkins. When he glanced at Lacey, he saw her sigh with a long-suffering expression.

He suddenly understood. "Venus, did you just spill your drink on me on purpose?"

She shrugged, unrepentant. "Well, of course, darlin', how else was I going to check you out and see if you're suitable for my best friend?"

"You see? This proves my point," Nate said between rueful chuckles as he blotted his wet jeans. "Women are much more devious about these things. A man would never intentionally spill a drink on his buddy's girl just to cop a feel."

Lacey's eyes widened. "Yes, a man most certainly would. Men invented the art! And she wasn't copping a feel."

"Sorry, Lacey," Raul said, his annoyance obvious. "I think he's right. She pretty much admitted she was copping a feel."

Lacey didn't even glance at him. "You stay out of this."

"Face it. Women are more manipulative than men," Nate said.

The Irish musicians who'd begun playing a few minutes earlier finished a set of tunes. The bar patrons who'd been listening applauded perfunctorily, not that the musicians cared. With karmic timing, the room descended into a moment of unexpected quiet.

Venus lifted a brow. "Who's manipulative? I was curious, that's all." She sat down and lounged back, looking not a bit sheepish. "I didn't imagine it would be exactly polite for me to ask if you had the package to keep satisfying my best friend here. Until she met you last week, she hadn't had a good lay in the three years I've known her."

The deafening silence held for another ten seconds beyond Venus's loud observation. It was followed by a roar of laughter from the table behind them. Nate watched as Lacey, calm, professional, put-together Lacey, dropped her forehead to the table in front of her, raised one hand and yelled, "Check, please."

THOUGH SHE'D NEVER done it in the entire time she'd worked at *For Her Eyes Only*, Lacey took what Raul called a "slick" day the next day. She wasn't really sick, not in the technical sense of the word. But she did feel queasy every time she thought of the awful scene at the pub.

She couldn't imagine what Nate must have thought about Venus's typically outrageous comment. Lacey had made an excuse—which no one bought—right afterward and left the bar. Venus had insisted on walking her to her car, to apologize. Though, in typical Venus style, she didn't really see that what she'd done was so awful.

Venus had been completely charmed by the man, which wasn't saying much, since Venus could be charmed by any man who was gorgeous and laughed at her jokes. Still, something Venus had said when she'd walked Lacey to her car remained with Lacey long into the night. "You come alive with him, Lacey. The way you look at him, and the way he looks at you, both of you trying to hide it, but it was like there was no one else in the place, like the two of you were in your own world somewhere and the rest of us were completely excluded." Then, with typical Venus bluntness, she said, "Pissed me off, to be perfectly honest."

Lacey had thought about it all night, knowing it was true. There was definitely something happening between her and Nate Logan. It seemed impossible, didn't fit in with what she knew about herself, what she planned for herself.

Since she'd moved to Baltimore, Lacey had struggled to be the person everyone wanted her to be. Her mother and stepfather wanted the subdued, conservative, soft-spoken daughter they'd tried to form during her childhood. Her real father wanted the driven, successful journalist to prove to the world that his genes would carry on through her. Her boss and colleagues wanted the conscientious, serious writer who could help them all by improving their circulation. Raul wanted a big sister. Venus wanted a confidante and a playmate.

In the dark, lonely night, Lacey admitted to herself that the only times she'd felt real lately were when she'd been battling Nate Logan on the pages of the magazine. And during those wonderful moments in her father's deserted gym Friday night. Their laughter in the pool, their connection while she'd bandaged him. Their passion on the trampoline. Oh, yes, that had indeed made her feel real. Like she'd finally found the place she belonged. The place she'd been searching for since finding out her parents had been lying to her for the first twelve years of her life.

The confused thoughts muddying her brain were enough to give anyone a sleepless night. So Tuesday morning Lacey called her office, faked a cold and went back to bed with a pint of Häagen Dazs Rum Raisin.

"Milk. Fruit. It's breakfast food," she muttered as she dug into the ice cream and turned on the television. A quick flip of the channels offered the usual weekday-morning fare—the wild and outrageous on the talk shows, the clueless and greedy on the game shows, the disgustingly perky on the morning shows and the dour and depressing on the world news. She turned the TV off.

After eating her fill of ice cream, Lacey put it away,

consoling herself that she really hadn't devoured an entire six-hundred-calorie pint all by herself. There were, after all, at least two spoonfuls stuck to the bottom and sides of the container.

Deciding to do some work in her home office, Lacey took a quick shower and pulled on some stretchy shorts and an old, ratty T-shirt. "One benefit of working at home," she said as she went into the second bedroom of her apartment, where she had a fairly decent computer system.

Just after she'd turned on her computer, Lacey heard a knock at her front door. Glancing at her watch, she saw it was nearly ten and knew it couldn't be Venus, who had a job interview this morning. When she reached her door and peeked through the peephole, she half expected to see the mailman with a package. Instead she saw a blond hunk with dimples.

"Oh, no, please," she muttered and thunked her forehead against the door.

"Come on, Lacey, I heard you. I know you're there."

Resigned, Lacey tugged the door open, half hiding behind it and wishing she'd bothered to at least put on a shirt without any holes in it. "How did you find out where I live?"

"Raul. How else?"

Lacey pictured Raul strapped down to various devices formerly used by Spanish inquisitors. "What do you want?"

"I heard you were sick," Nate said as he breezed past her into her apartment without waiting for an invitation. "I brought comfort food." He held up a brown paper bag.

"Chicken soup?" she asked skeptically.

"Brownies."

"You can stay," Lacey said as she grabbed the bag out of his hand and carried it into the kitchen. *Hmm, brownies. Flour and eggs to go with the milk and fruit.*

Nate followed her, taking a quick glance around her apartment. It was decorated in simple bright colors with lots of house plants and photographs. Not ritzy, not expensive, as he might have expected for the daughter of a multimillionaire. But nice, classy and elegant, much like Lacey herself. "So are you really sick?"

"Sick in the head for letting you in," she retorted.

"Look, I'm sorry about last night. But you can't exactly blame me for your friend's big, huge mouth."

Lacey shrugged as she opened the brownies. She wasted no time with plates or napkins, pulling out the biggest piece and biting right into it. "I know. It's not your fault. Venus is, uh, somewhat unpredictable," she mumbled between bites.

"I liked her." Nate noted her resigned shrug.

"Most men do."

He clarified. "I said I liked her. I wasn't attracted to her." He stepped closer, until he stood within touching distance of Lacey. She took a tiny, tentative step back but couldn't go far because of the kitchen table behind her.

"None of my business if you were," she said, her voice not much more than a whisper.

"Of course it is."

She cleared her throat and glanced away. "Why is that?"

Nate stepped closer, until the toe of his shoe was even with the ends of her pretty rose-tinted toenails. Tipping her chin with his finger, he forced her to look at him and note the seriousness of his words. "Because you're the one who has some serious misconceptions about who I am and what I'm like. Contrary to what you might think from my column, I'm not the type of man who would chase after the woman sitting *next* to me when I really want the one sitting *across* from me."

Turning her head away, she swallowed nervously. He watched the movement in her throat and remembered how her skin tasted there, right there, in that sweet hollow.

"You're speaking metaphorically, right?"

He shook his head. "I haven't felt a serious attraction for any woman for a long time. Except one."

Nate watched as a flush came to her cheeks. She looked much as she had in the robe Friday night—hair damp, no makeup. Dressed in shorts and a T-shirt that had definitely seen better days, she was still beautiful to him. She took another nervous nibble of her brownie, obviously not ready to have this conversation. Too bad. It was overdue. "We can't avoid this, Lacey. What's more, I don't *want* to avoid this."

"Avoid what?"

Nate leaned closer, staring into her beautiful face, counting those freckles, getting lost in those blue eyes. "Avoid you and me. What happened." He lowered his voice. "What *else* is going to happen."

She had a tiny crumb of brownie on the corner of one lip, and as his stare zeroed in on it, she licked it away, catching the crumb with her pink tongue. He had to close his eyes as the memory of how she tasted, how her mouth felt when joined to his, invaded his mind. He took a deep breath, catching the sweet rose scent that was so uniquely hers.

When he opened his eyes, he saw her biting her lip, staring just as intently at him. Her face so easily gave her emotions away—nervousness, anxiety and mistrust warred with the same siren's call of attraction to which they'd both succumbed Friday.

"What else is going to happen, Nate?" Her whispered question revealed her confusion, and her need.

Caught up in the same feelings he'd had when they were together on the trampoline, Nate repeated his first prediction. "Something amazing."

Glancing lower, he noticed a hole in her shirt below her right collarbone. Remembering kissing her in that exact spot a few nights before, he was unable to resist a slow, lazy smile. Though he waited for her to duck away or turn around, she didn't move an inch as he lifted his hand to the front of her shirt. "It's torn," he whispered. Moving the tip of his index finger to the small hole, he rubbed the soft cotton, then lightly brushed the softer skin beneath.

She gasped in reaction. But still she didn't move away.

"How can you look more beautiful to me now than you did when I first saw you in the gym Friday night?" he asked, hearing bemusement in his voice and knowing she heard it, too. He continued his tender exploration of the tiny amount of flesh revealed by her shirt, the smoothness of her skin accentuated by the roughness of his.

She moaned. As he watched, her head fell back and her eyes closed. Lacey's sweetly curved lips parted and her breath deepened as she asked, "How can I want you so much when I don't like you?" Her voice held a note of desperation.

Nate didn't answer right away, instead doing what he'd wanted to do since he'd walked in the door. He slipped his fingers into her hair, fingering its damp silkiness, then tugged her closer. Her eyes flew open, though she didn't pull away. Before he took her mouth with his, Nate whispered, "You just don't know me yet."

Then her lips met his, frantically opening, kissing him back, meeting his tongue with the sweetness of hers. Nate slipped one hand lower, to tug her closer, while the other remained tangled in her hair. Breaths mingled, sighs became moans, and Nate fell headfirst into the maelstrom of intensity and desire he'd felt with Lacey when they'd met.

Their kisses were sweeter now. Sweeter because she knew who she was kissing...and kissed him anyway. Sweeter because he knew who he was kissing...and wanted her that much more for it.

"This is... I can't..."

"Shh," he whispered against her lips. And she did, sighing in surrender as she slipped her arms around his shoulders. Her fingers moved beneath the cotton of his shirt, brushing against his sensitized skin. His body reacted, driving toward her, and she met his instinctive thrust, pressing herself tightly against him from shoulder to hip.

She didn't object when he lifted her by the waist and sat her on her sturdy butcher-block kitchen table. She kept kissing him, holding his shoulders, then his hair.

Nate wanted her closer. Cupping her hips, he tugged her forward on the table. Moving his hands to her thighs, he gently pulled them apart and stepped between them.

"What...oh," she said with a sigh as he stepped between her legs, pressing himself against her heat. The hard ridge of his erection, throbbing against his jeans, met the sweet warmth between her thighs. She moaned again, and her body jerked hard against him.

"I've wanted to touch you like this since the minute I saw you," he said, his voice hoarse as sensation washed over him and his body demanded more.

She curled her fingers into his hair and pulled him close for another one of those slow, wet kisses that made him lose his mind. One of her long legs curled around his hips as she leaned back on the table, tugging him down with her.

"This isn't supposed to happen," she whispered when he moved his mouth to her neck. "Our assignment. The story..."

"Do you really care about the story right now?"

She shook her head, closing her eyes as he lifted her cotton shirt and stroked the smooth skin of her stomach. "I can't make my brain work at all when you're touching me like this."

Nate knew what she meant. It was overwhelming, intoxicating, this urgency between them. It had been like this from the beginning. Intense. Demanding. Instinctive. Thought played no part. That, unfortunately, was the problem. *Thought is playing no part.* Though it nearly killed him, Nate dropped her shirt and eased his body back so they weren't so intimately pressed together.

Lacey immediately felt him pull away. "What's wrong?" she asked, her brow furrowing in confusion and disappointment.

He ran a frustrated hand through his hair and shook his head hard, as if to clear it. "I might have to shoot myself later for saying this, but...damn, Lacey, I *want* your brain involved in this decision."

Of all the things Lacey might have imagined hearing

coming out of Nate Logan's mouth at a moment like this, that wasn't one of them. "You...you want my brain involved?"

A tender smile crossed those amazing lips she'd curled her tongue over moments before. "Yeah. We both know what our bodies want. Maybe we should give our minds a chance to catch up."

Lacey slowly sat up, her legs dangling off the edge of the table. Bracing her palms on the wood surface, she took a few deep breaths as she studied his face. His words were light and simple, but she read more in his expression. There was need there. Heat, emotion and unfulfilled desire.

She'd been his for the asking. He knew it as well as she did. And he'd been as ready as she had—still was, if the obvious bulge in his jeans was any indication. Yet he'd stopped. "You know, if a woman had done what you just did, she'd be called a tease."

"I'm not trying to tease you, Lacey," he replied. "I'm dying to finish what we started." As if to illustrate that fact, he stepped closer until his straining zipper brushed against her leg. She shivered. "But not at the risk of it having no meaning."

Lacey watched him wait for her decision. She came close, so damn close, to grabbing him by the shoulders and pulling him down onto the table. The choice was in her hands. He'd stepped back to let her breathe, let her think, let her brain *engage*.

It did. Damn.

Mentally acknowledging she was not going to pull him back down on top of her, Lacey didn't know whether to thank him or smack him. Nate obviously saw her decision. He stepped to the sink, bent over and splashed some water on his face.

By the time he turned around, Lacey had slid off the table, nearly groaning as she tugged her cotton shorts away from the achingly tender, wet flesh between her thighs. Her entire body thrummed with energy, wanting to strain toward him, needing the release he could provide. She remained still.

"I guess we should get to work on the assignment," she said softly. "This would have...well, it would have been..." *Amazingly perfect? Beyond imagination?* "...awkward."

Nate didn't move toward her, simply turned and met her eyes from the other side of the kitchen. "No, Lacey." His intensity unnerved her as he let his gaze travel over her entire body, from swollen lips to shaky legs. "It would have been just as incredible as it was Friday night. Maybe even better. Better than either one of us has been fantasizing about since the minute we met."

Then he turned and walked out the door.

6

NATE LOGAN starred in Lacey's dreams that night. Images of endless kisses, erotic touches and wildly seductive positions filled the long, dark hours. She was finally shaken awake by a shockingly intense orgasm that forced her to sit up in bed to catch her breath, wondering what the hell had happened!

The possibility of climaxing in her sleep had never even occurred to her. Then again, Lacey hadn't exactly had a great deal of sexual experience. Until last Friday, with Nate, she'd only ever had a sum total of three boyfriends. Sex had been involved in only one of those three relationships. Not horrible sex, but not great sex, either, which had helped Lacey realize she hadn't really loved him. All in all, she'd been left unfulfilled and confused about the whole concept of a mind-blowing orgasm. She'd felt nothing that came even close to mind-blowing. Since she'd also never felt completely comfortable taking care of things herself, Lacey figured she'd just wait for her soul mate to make the earth move for her.

Nate Logan was definitely not her soul mate. *So how did he make the earth move? Not just Friday, but in my dreams?*

"He didn't," she told herself, ending the mental argument. "Friday night was bound to happen after having no sex for such a long time. Could have happened with anyone!" As for her dreams, well…they were just dreams. The fact that he'd starred in them was irrelevant. They were simply a little gift from her subconscious to her body. Her reaction wasn't so surprising since she'd been on the edge for days.

Okay, yes, dammit, she'd admit one thing, Nate had *put* her on the edge. So much so that she had been highly tempted to do some experimenting on her own, if only to relieve the intense need in her body. She wanted him, no question about it. Wanted his mouth and his hands, not to mention his deliciously hard…

"Knock it off," she muttered as she threw herself onto her pillow and willed sleep to come. And if she intentionally tried to lose herself in the same dream— well, no one would know in the morning light, would they?

She fell asleep with a smile on her face.

THE NEXT DAY, Lacey heard from Nate via e-mail. He had some work to finish up on his columns and told her he planned to work at home for a few days to avoid distractions. He didn't say what type of distractions. Lacey had to wonder if he found her as distracting as she found him, but she wasn't about to ask.

Nate sent her frequent notes discussing his ideas for their assignment. He'd been thinking as much as she had. They'd each conduct interviews, do man-on-the-street opinion polls, look at pop culture views about the male-female relationship, plus contact a few celebrities for glitz factor.

He suggested going a step further, actual physical investigation. "A singles joint?" she scoffed as she read one message. He really thought the two of them should go to the same club, sit apart and do some research on how men and women interacted while seeking out members of the opposite sex?

Once she thought about it, she admitted the idea had some merit. But there was no way she was going for his next suggestion. "I am *not* answering a lonely hearts ad and going on a blind date," she typed. "But by all means, feel free to do that yourself. I'm sure there are plenty of single white females who'd love the chance to help Naughty Nate on a story."

Distracted by meetings for the rest of the morning, Lacey had forgotten about her message by the time she checked her e-mail that afternoon. When she opened his reply, she read "SWM seeks thong-wearing blonde for serious fun. Trampolines and pools involved. Sturdy kitchen table a must."

She shivered in her chair, wondering how she could make her want him and laugh at him with the same words. Of course, he'd been able to make her laugh from the very beginning. Yes, he was overconfident and had an abundance of charm, but his natural good humor was infectious. She'd never met a man like him.

She'd certainly never met a man who would have walked away from her in her kitchen the day before. A man who'd wanted her brain every bit as much as her body. While physically she'd felt like screaming in frustration, Lacey had been even more shocked by the feelings of tenderness his actions had inspired once she'd thought about them after he'd gone.

He'd cared about her too much to take what they were both panting for. He wanted her beyond one quick moment of release. So he'd stepped back. That certainly wasn't the action of a callous, insensitive, sexist man. Nothing Nate Logan had done from the minute they'd met had shown him to be anything other than a sexy, considerate, free-spirited charmer.

"He was right," she mumbled as she sat at her desk, staring unseeingly at the computer screen. "I never really knew him."

She hadn't known the real man by reading his columns any more than the average guy on the street knew her father from the media blitz surrounding his romantic escapades.

She'd begun to know Nate, though. And she liked him. Her feelings had already gone beyond attraction, beyond interest. That somehow made things worse. It had been bad enough having to work with him when she thought him despicable. Now, suspecting he was someone she could respect, even admire, their assignment would be sheer misery.

Because she couldn't have him. Lacey couldn't take what he offered—a joyful, sensual affair that might fulfill her physically but would leave her emotions tattered in the end.

She conceded Nate Logan was not a sexist jerk. Nor, however, was he the stick-around, committed type. Yes, he cared about her. Yes, he wanted more than a one-night stand. But how much more? A week? Six weeks? A few months? Surely no more than that. Certainly not a lifetime.

Getting involved with him would go against everything Lacey wrote about, everything she'd believed in since she was a child.

Since the nights when she'd hidden her head under her pillow while her mother and stepfather argued about her, she'd hoped that somewhere, someday, she'd find a man who would love her unconditionally, in spite of anything she ever did. And during the visits to her real father, when J.T. and his girlfriend du jour would entertain in wildly lavish style, she'd recognized deep down she wasn't like him, could never be like him, because she would never settle for less than true love. She wanted honesty, fidelity and trust—things most of the adults in her life had seemed to lack when she was growing up.

Dammit, she wanted happily ever after. She wanted her soul mate, her *Anam Cara,* her split apart.

"And I want Nate Logan," she admitted aloud, leaning back in her desk chair and sighing in frustration. At this particular moment, she honestly wasn't able to say which she wanted more.

BY WEDNESDAY at four, Nate knew he'd had enough. Fun e-mails were one thing, but he really wanted to see Lacey again. Calling her at the office, he waited until she answered, then said, "My car needs washing."

"Nate?"

"Yep. Let's get to work, Lace. There's a self-serve car wash a few blocks from the office. Meet me there."

"Forget it. I'm wearing a silk blouse."

He paused for a quick mental image of her in a wet silk blouse. A white one. A very sheer white one. That might be even better than a T-shirt.

Lacey didn't notice his silence. "How about the library?"

Nate groaned. "It's a beautiful, sunny afternoon and you want to bury us in the city library?"

She paused. "Have any dirty clothes?"

"Of course, the Laundromat," he agreed.

They met an hour later at the agreed-upon location—a Laundromat in a strip mall in Towson. Lacey looked somewhat out of place, dressed in an ivory-colored business suit, the silk blouse—green—and a string of pearls. Nate, with his faded, torn jeans and dingy Orioles shirt, fit right in. "Wanna help me sort my whites?"

She glanced at his laundry basket and raised a droll brow. "I'm sure sorting your whites would be the highlight of my week. But, no, I think we should separate if we really want to observe the swinging single scene at the Laundromat."

He knew she was right. But separate wasn't what he had in mind. Actually, now that he had Lacey in a hot, sweaty Laundromat filled with dozens of heavy-duty, industrial-strength, *vibrating* washing machines, being separate was the last thing on his mind! He couldn't think of a good enough reason to get her to sit on top of one of the things, however, and watched helplessly while she went clear across the room and sat in a corner near the front windows.

Lacey perched on the cracked edge of an ancient metal folding chair, whose seat had once been orange, and had once been cushioned. Within forty minutes three men hit on her. None of them looked like Prince Charming—more like the prince's ninety-year-old toothless stablehands, or the dirty storybook villains who locked the princess away in the tower.

Judging by the pinched frown on her face, Nate knew Lacey was not amused by their people-watching in the Laundromat. Nate didn't fare much better. Yes, he definitely got some attention from the females entering the place. Most, however, *weren't* young singles on the make. They were harried housewives with runny-nosed two-year-olds glued to their hips, or older women who looked like they needed to start measuring their bra size in length instead of circumference. After an hour, he was ready to call it quits. "This was a bad idea."

"I figured since we're near the university, we might hit some of the college crowd," Lacey admitted with a sigh.

"So maybe next time we try the college library instead?"

"You're on. Now, let's get out of here. I'm feeling the need to take a shower after being around all this dirty laundry."

Nate chalked up their Laundromat experience as a draw.

BY THE END of Thursday, Lacey had really begun to look forward to Nate's e-mails, especially since at the bottom he always included something irreverent or outrageous to amuse her. From lame dumb blonde jokes—What do you call a blonde skeleton in the closet? The all-time-hide-and-seek champion!—to cuttingly hilarious political commentary, he somehow managed to put a grin on her face with each note.

On Friday, he sent her a link to a Web article about a woman who'd discovered her husband of eighteen years was a cross-dresser who liked to impersonate Madonna. Lacey grimaced as she read it. By the time she was done, she had another message from him. "Bet she thought he was *charming* when they first met."

Remembering his comment about her Prince Charming being fictional or gay, Lacey chuckled. Then she fired back. "I thought *you* were charming when we met."

Twenty minutes later he'd sent her an attachment. A smiley face with a bandage over its head. And the words, "Ouch. That hurt worse than the chair."

In return, Lacey sent him a link to an Internet article about a cheating man whose wife and two girlfriends had teamed up to feed him small amounts of arsenic over several months.

He replied, "You asking me to dinner?"

"I can't cook," she replied electronically.

Five minutes later the phone rang. "I can cook."

She smiled into the receiver. "Nate?"

"You sending sassy e-mails to some other guy who can cook?"

"I wasn't hinting around for a dinner invitation."

"You've got one anyway. I make the meanest spaghetti in the city." When she didn't respond immediately, he cajoled her. "And did I ever tell you that I live right around the corner from an Italian bakery? They've got pastries that'll make you beg."

If she was crazy enough to spend an evening alone with Nate in his apartment, Lacey had a feeling it wouldn't be pastries she'd be begging for. "I don't know...."

"Come on, I'll finish up my other project this morning. You can come later this afternoon, we'll work, have an early dinner, and you'll still be home by nine."

They did have to get to work. The further Lacey got with the background interviews on this project, the more she realized she and Nate needed to coordinate on some topics, not to mention set some ground rules for their stories.

Not quite believing she was going to do it, she took a deep breath and said, "Okay. I'll come."

NATE GOT READY for Lacey's visit the same way he would have prepared if his parents were coming to town. That meant folding the mountain of clean laundry on his sofa and running the vacuum that usually only collected whatever dust landed on it, not to mention stashing the spoils of his freelance work.

In recent months, Nate had managed to accumulate a huge amount of goodies while researching articles he wrote for publications outside his *Men's World* day job. Much of the stuff he gave to friends or family members. The women's items, however, had been piling up. A week ago, he'd read about a local shelter looking for donations. Thrilled to finally have a place to hand off the makeup, magazines, books, feminine products and beauty supplies he'd received while writing articles for women's weeklies, he'd planned to box it all up and haul it out this weekend.

"No time now," he muttered as he scrambled to shove things out of the way before Lacey's arrival. He didn't really want to have to explain the case of tampons in his bathroom. Particularly given what she already thought of him!

He couldn't wait to see her again. It had been hell staying away from the office, not giving in to his urge to call her. Until now, he'd only allowed himself to e-mail her because they really did have to stay in touch. At least with the computer notes they didn't have to deal with this physical pull between them but it was still there, humming away right beneath the surface of his skin, threatening to drive him nuts if he didn't act on it soon. But not too soon. Not before she was ready to trust him, to trust what was happening. Not before she had a chance to decide with her brain as well as her body.

So e-mail was the only communication he allowed himself. With each message, he sensed her reserve dropping, her confidence building. Yes, they were working well on the story. Now he needed to show her how well they could work personally.

He'd told her to come around four, so when he heard a knock at three forty-five, Nate panicked. He hadn't showered yet, and he was right in the middle of making the sauce.

"You said spaghetti," Lacey said when he opened the door. She held up a bottle of red wine. Nate watched as she looked him over, head to toe, obviously noting the tomato sauce on his shirt, the worn jeans and his bare feet. She bit her lip. "I guess I'm early. I'm not familiar with this neighborhood, and these brownstones all look alike. I was afraid I'd get lost."

She looked adorably disconcerted. Ah, hell, just plain adorable. He didn't think he'd ever seen her in jeans, but, oh, the woman had the figure for them. Not to mention the dark green, clingy sleeveless tank top she wore with them. She'd obviously gone home to change. Nate couldn't imagine her going to work dressed so casually. Not to mention so damned sexily, though she probably didn't even realize that. Most women had the mistaken impression that men only thought clothes cut down to there or slit up to here were sexy. As if skin had to show for a man to be interested.

As far as Nate was concerned, nothing made a woman look as good as a clingy top that hugged every curve and a pair of jeans tight enough to outline the fine curve of her sweet...

"Nate?"

"Uh, sorry," he muttered. "It's okay. I was running late myself—I'd planned the world's fastest shower."

"Sorry. Should I come back?"

He held the door open and stepped back. "Come on

in and make yourself at home. I've got to finish in the kitchen, or we'll never be able to eat. Then I'll get cleaned up. Okay?"

Nodding, she followed him into the apartment, looking around approvingly. The heels of her flat sandals clicked on the mellowed oak floors, and he saw her smile as she noticed the bench seat in the bay window overlooking the street. "This place is great. So much character. Much better than my complex."

"Yeah, I like it. The wiring's archaic, and you have to pray no one in the building flushes a toilet while you're taking a shower, but it's got a hell of a lot of charm." Nate went into the kitchen and got to work chopping onions and peppers.

She joined him. "Have you lived here long?"

"Nah. I moved up from Virginia less than a year ago."

Nate had loved this area of old Baltimore from the first time he'd visited his sister and her husband two years before. When he got the job at *Men's World*, there was no question about where he wanted to live. Kelsey and Mitch had invited him to take one of the apartments in their renovated building, but Nate had refused. That would be a bit too much like the way they'd grown up, with Nate and his best friend, Mitch, getting into all sorts of scrapes and his little sister, Kelsey, tagging along behind causing even more trouble.

Dumping the vegetables in a pan with a small amount of olive oil, he sautéed them and then scraped them into the pot of simmering tomato sauce. "My sister and her husband live in another brownstone a few blocks away. They've renovated theirs. Mitch makes considerably more money writing college textbooks than I do ladling out advice for guys who haven't had a date since the Reagan administration."

She chuckled. "Are you and your sister close?"

"Always were. It helped that she married my best friend." He gave a rueful shake of his head. "Mitch never had a chance."

"Sounds like there's a story there."

Laughing at the way his determined sister had roped herself a man, Nate said, "I want you to meet her sometime. As a matter of fact, I've already told her about you."

She looked surprised. "Really? Why?"

"Let's say she's definitely someone who can help us with this assignment we're working on. She's got a lot of connections, knows a lot of people and has a very cool job."

Opening the bottle of wine Lacey had brought, Nate splashed a helping into the pot of sauce and stirred it. "Perfect choice. Want a glass now?"

"It's a bit early for me." She accepted the glass of water he offered instead. "Sounds like your relationship with your sister is great. You also have a younger brother, right?"

"Yep. The baby of the family," Nate replied as he finished stirring the sauce and put the lid on the pot. "A spoiled little punk, but he'll grow out of it, I'm sure. What about you?"

She nodded. "Two younger brothers."

Nate didn't suppose J.T. had any more children running around, but he had to ask. "Uh, whole brothers?"

"No. Are you asking because you're interested or because that reporter's instinct is kicking in?"

"I told you I wouldn't say anything, Lace." He shrugged as he started washing pans. "I was just curious. I mean, it's not every day in this paparazzi-loaded world that a man like J.T. can keep his only child a secret."

"He didn't know about me until I was twelve," she admitted.

Lacey watched Nate clean up the kitchen, enjoying, as always, his refreshing self-confidence. Here he was, barefoot, with specks of tomato sauce on his clothes, cooking and waiting on her, yet looking every bit the gorgeous, masculine man he was. Again she sensed that uncanny ability of his to be comfortable in his own skin, at ease with whatever role he played. She admired that. Envied it, in fact.

"How did he find out?"

Believing he was seriously interested, not trying to pry, she said, "I wrote him a letter asking him if he was my father."

Nate blinked. "You're kidding."

"No, I'm not."

"What made you think he was your father? I mean, it sounds like a fairy tale—the woodcutter's daughter learns she's the lost princess or something."

She smiled slightly, remembering feeling exactly that way a few times during her teen years when she'd struggled so hard to make sense of her world. "I overheard my parents arguing one night." She shrugged, then continued. "About me, as usual."

"They argued a lot?"

"No, not a lot. But whenever they did, it was usually because of something I'd done. I used to tell myself it was because I was the oldest, because my two younger brothers were boys and my father liked his sons better than his daughter."

"I'm the oldest of three, too," Nate interjected when she paused. "I know all about always getting blamed."

"I guess I deserved the blame sometimes. I think that argument was over me getting caught throwing water balloons off the roof of the general store at people in the parking lot."

"Water balloons. How shocking for a twelve-year-old."

"Well, we *had* put food coloring in the water."

"Uh-oh."

"Mrs. Ulster, the children's resource officer from the library, wasn't happy about her white poodle turning green."

He chuckled.

"Not to mention her hair."

"Ouch."

Remembering the rest of the story, Lacey admitted, "I guess the worst part was that we didn't have balloons, so my best friend had stolen a box of condoms from her brother's room. She saw it in an old movie once. They worked pretty well."

Nate let out a bark of laughter. "That must have been a sight."

"Oh, yes. I think Mrs. Ulster would have been fine about the green hair if it hadn't been for the fact that a rubber got stuck to her earring and kind of hung there for a while before anyone pointed it out to her."

Nate dropped to a chair next to her, laughing so hard she saw tears come to his eyes. Lacey was able to shake her head in rueful amusement at the memory.

"When you're the daughter of the most respected pastor in town, it doesn't do to let the sheriff catch you and your girlfriends running around throwing water-bomb condoms at people," she continued matter-of-factly.

"I suppose not."

"Anyway, that night I overheard more than I should have when my parents argued about it. He was so angry, I really thought he might walk out. And I found out the disinterest I'd always sensed from my father was because I wasn't really his daughter at all."

"What'd you do?"

"I asked my mother about it the next day, but she wouldn't tell me the truth. Instead, she begged me to be good, to be the kind of daughter any man would be proud to claim, so our family would be okay."

Nate's laughter faded. "Heavy load."

She nodded. "For the first time I realized I could be responsible for breaking my parents apart. So I decided to try to do better."

Nate reached across the table and smoothed a stray wisp of hair off her forehead, his touch tender.

"But of course," Lacey continued once he'd moved his hand away, "I wasn't giving up on who my father was. Like any preteen acting purely on hormones and instinct, I snooped through my mother's memory box and found a newspaper photo of her and J.T. It was dated the year I was born. So I wrote to him."

"That's a hell of a lot for a twelve-year-old to take on," he said, crossing his arms in front of his chest. His usual flirtatious grin wasn't playing about those curved lips. Instead he looked sympathetic, even understanding. "I imagine the proverbial you-know-what hit the fan?"

She laughed and nodded. "Oh, you bet. It took a few months while J.T.'s private investigators snooped into my background, then he finally showed up at my parents' house demanding to meet me."

"Ouch."

"Double ouch. It was during the ladies' church auxiliary club meeting, right in our living room, with my stepfather the pastor as special guest. I don't even remember what story my mother told to get everyone out of the house."

"And how did little Lacey react?"

"Much as you'd expect the lost princess in the woodcutter's shack to react. I came downstairs with my suitcase packed, ready to skip out of Smeltsville, Indiana, forever." Lacey sighed at the memory of her mother's tearstained face. "Twelve-year-olds can be incredibly self-absorbed."

Nate must have sensed her sudden doubt. He crouched next to her chair and took her hand. "You were one amazing kid."

She stared at their entwined fingers, the contact bringing to mind the sensations and emotions of Friday night and Tuesday morning. She suddenly found she'd lost her train of thought.

Nate followed her stare, then pulled his hand free and walked to his seat. "But somehow your parents kept the secret, no one found out, and the princess didn't go off to live in the palace," he said, reminding her of the subject at hand and obviously trying to get past the moment of intense awareness between them.

"J.T. told my mother he wouldn't drag her into court or fight for custody if she'd agree to a blood test and then some form of visitation," Lacey explained. "So, starting that next summer, I would go away for two weeks, to *camp* as far as everyone but my parents knew. And I was forbidden to discuss it with anyone, not even my brothers."

"They don't know?" he asked.

"Andrew does. He's in college now. My youngest brother, Jake, still doesn't."

Nate frowned. "I can't imagine parents asking a twelve-year-old to lie to the entire world, including her own brothers, for years on end."

"It was hardest with my grandparents. My stepfather's parents," she clarified. "I'm very close to them."

"Talk about a different atmosphere," Nate continued, shaking his head. "From minister's angel to the daughter of a millionaire playboy."

Lacey gave a rueful laugh. "Definite culture shock. Camp J.T. involved foreign vacations, presents and parties. A whirlwind fantasy, which I would enjoy right up until I got homesick for my mother, grandparents and brothers, right around day thirteen when it was time for me to pack to go home."

"I bet J.T. supplied as many water balloons as you wanted, and probably helped you throw them."

Lacey shrugged. "J.T. would have let me get away with just about anything. Unfortunately, he was child enough for both of us. All his scrapes, his affairs—well, when I was with him I felt like he needed some stable family time."

He didn't respond for a minute, then slowly nodded as he absorbed what she'd said. As for Lacey, she couldn't quite believe she'd said it. She'd spilled the entire story of her childhood to a man to whom she wouldn't have given the time of day a week ago. This was *so* not her. Then again, everything she'd done since the moment she met Nate Logan was so not her.

"Okay, now you know my life history, which is way more than you needed to hear."

"Is it so tough to trust me?" Nate asked, his green eyes shining with friendly interest.

No. No, it hadn't been. She found that downright amazing. She did trust him. Oh, boy, now she was getting in deep. First wild attraction, then true liking, and now trust? Good grief, she'd better be careful or she'd find herself falling crazy in love with the man! Which definitely wouldn't fit into her plans to find a gentle, nurturing soul mate.

"I suppose not," she admitted.

"I'm glad you did. I think I see things more clearly now."

Though she raised a questioning brow, he didn't elaborate.

"Tell you what," he said. "Make yourself at home. I'm going to go take a shower, okay?"

Still confused by the feelings she'd finally begun to acknowledge, Lacey nodded. After he left, she took her water glass, went into the living area of the apartment and sat on the cream-colored leather sofa. She leaned back in the seat but quickly leaped up, a screech on her lips, when she felt something poke her in the small of her back. Reaching behind the cushion, she felt the cool, smooth, tube-shaped object that had poked her. Pulling it free, she saw it was a curling iron, similar to the one in her bathroom.

Lacey frowned. Nate's hair was short. And he sure didn't seem the type of man to worry about the perfect do.

Brushing aside her idle curiosity, Lacey placed the appliance on the coffee table, next to a carton filled with magazines. When she looked closer she realized they were all women's magazines. *Cosmo, Elle, Marie-Claire*—current issues of at least half a dozen ladies' monthlies. "He's a journalist. He's just checking out the competition," Lacey muttered, trying to convince herself.

The makeup was harder to understand. Beneath a table near the front door stood a packing carton. Even from here she could see the tubes and vials filling it to the brim. She recognized the Cover Girl packaging and other brands as well. Lipsticks, nail polish, powders and eyeshadows. "Why on earth is he ordering makeup?" Figuring maybe he'd taken a shipment for his sister or something, Lacey shrugged, stood up and walked around.

Within a few minutes, she realized she hadn't asked Nate if he had a powder room—and she needed one. Spotting a couple of closed doors near an arched hallway, she crossed her fingers and pulled one open. Instead of a bathroom, she found a coat closet...without a single coat in sight.

"Lingerie?" The closet was crowded with padded hangers bearing absolutely delicious lingerie. She couldn't help touching it. She reached out and fingered the fine fabric of a lovely plum-colored teddy with matching short robe. All lace and silk, it slid across her fingers like liquid. On the next two hangers, a white cotton nightdress looked like cool comfort, and a black lacy bustier and garter belt screamed Frederick's of Hollywood.

Lacey's secret addiction to sexy underclothes left her mouth watering as she examined each and every item. Robes, peignoirs, teddies in several shades—the closet was a veritable feast of lacy, frilly, fantasy lingerie. All new, tagged, fresh and unworn.

"He's either a crossdresser or a complete reprobate," she muttered out loud.

She didn't notice Nate walking up the hallway until his hand covered hers on the door of the closet. Startled, she jumped and turned to find him chuckling.

"Or," he said softly, "just a man with very good taste."

7

LACEY FELT a flush stain her cheeks as she realized Nate had caught her being nosy. "I'm sorry. I was checking to see if this was the bathroom."

"Second door on the left," Nate said as he tilted his head, gesturing toward the short hallway leading to the back of the apartment. He waited, not making any effort to explain the contents of his closet. Considering she'd been the one caught snooping, Lacey didn't necessarily blame him.

Her intense curiosity warred with her embarrassment as he stood there, watching her shift from foot to foot and curl her fingers together nervously. She saw laughter in his eyes, and a seductive smile tugged at his lips. *Don't ask! Don't ask!*

To escape his amused eyes, Lacey tried to walk past him. He blocked most of the entrance into the hall, and she paused, waiting for him to move. He stayed right where he was, inches from where she stood, so close she could feel his warm breath in the cool, air-conditioned air.

Lacey tried not to notice the drops of water hanging from his hair and dripping onto the white towel he wore over his broad, bare shoulders. One drop trickled down his neck, riding on a cord of muscle. She watched it until it disappeared into the light hair on his chest. *No doubt about it, the guy works out,* she thought, noting the perfect symmetry of his form.

He wore only a pair of tight jeans. His feet were bare, as was his broad, sculpted chest. Lacey swallowed hard as her stare came to rest on his thick upper arms. He lifted the towel to his head, ran it across his damp hair, and she watched the ripple of muscles beneath his taut skin.

Finally, he took a step to the side to allow her to pass. The laughter had faded from his eyes. Now he stared at her intently. He had obviously noticed her scrutiny, and she watched him suck in a deep breath, then let it out on a shaky sigh.

Stepping quickly by him, her arm brushed his as she passed. Her skin tingled at the contact. Nearly breathless, she forced herself into the bathroom and shut the door behind her.

She needed to splash some cool water on her face. Her temperature had skyrocketed when her arm had so briefly touched Nate's. She'd had a shockingly vivid image of herself wearing the plum-colored teddy. For him.

Stop it, she told herself. She wasn't going to be sleeping with Nate Logan. This was a working dinner. A meeting with a colleague. An interesting, delectable colleague...who happened to have some rather bizarre items in his apartment.

Glancing around for a towel to dry her face and not seeing one, she reached over to open the door of a small linen closet. She spotted a stack of neatly folded towels, but her attention was firmly caught by a box on the floor of the closet. Inside the box were several very distinctive packages.

"Tampons?" And there was more. The guy had

every type of feminine hygiene product on the market. Lacey didn't believe what she was seeing at first. "Good grief, he's some kind of Lothario!" she murmured in shock. Only a man *very* accustomed to female houseguests would feel the need to stock up on such inarguably female products. And lingerie. And makeup.

Lacey rubbed a hand over her eyes, wondering which Nate to believe in. The one who'd amused her, who'd refused to take advantage of her, who'd listened to the story of her childhood with understanding and sympathy? Or the one who looked equipped to have the Baltimore Ravens' cheerleaders over for the weekend?

When she walked out of the bathroom a few minutes later, Lacey found Nate standing a few feet away in the doorway of another room. He hadn't noticed her. He was busy pulling a navy blue polo shirt over his head, tugging the fabric to fit over his thick arms and chest. Lacey watched silently, trying to figure him out.

When he turned and caught her staring at him suspiciously, an obvious grin appeared on his lips. His eyes crinkled at the corners. He laughed, a chuckle at first, then a rumble that rolled out of his chest.

"What's so funny?"

He didn't answer. Instead, he turned and walked into a nearby bedroom. When he flipped on a light, she saw the room was an office with a computer station and stacks of books and magazines. She wasn't a bit surprised to see a free-weight bench in one corner. "Nate?"

He continued to ignore her as he squatted next to a short bookcase and began pulling magazines off the shelf. He quickly glanced through one after another, discarding most into a pile at his feet. She heard him mutter something under his breath and asked, "What was that?"

"January oh-one," he said, but didn't explain.

Finally, curious, she entered the room and walked up behind him. After all the unusual items she'd spotted in his home, romance novels came as no big surprise. She noticed two sensual books by one of her favorite authors and several others stacked in a pile on the floor beneath the window.

Nate, meanwhile, continued to search for something. He was digging through back issues of old magazines, from *Playboy* to *Mountain Climber's Weekly*. "Aha!" he exclaimed as he stood, triumphantly holding one of the magazines. "January oh-one. Here."

Nate flipped through the issue. Folding back a page, he handed it to her. Lacey glanced down and caught the headline—"A Man's Guide to Those Pesky Feminine Products." Nate Logan's name was prominent beneath the heading.

"Oh, my goodness," she said with a grin as she understood what he was showing her. "And the lingerie?"

"Last May. Oh, I did love that article," he replied, a note of nostalgia in his voice.

"The makeup?"

"A few months ago," he replied, bending over to examine the magazines. "You'd be amazed how many men have no idea what women have to go through to put on eyeliner."

"The curling iron?" she asked, not even needing the answer.

"You found it? I was packing all that stuff up the other day. Today, when you said you'd come, I did a hurry-up cleaning job and shoved the boxes wherever I could stuff them. Couldn't find that curling iron, though."

She grinned. "It poked me in the back when I sat on the couch. I assume it's not yours?"

"Same article as the makeup, called 'What She Goes Through For You.' It's about how women prepare for a date. How on earth do you females bring yourselves to pluck your eyebrows?" He followed her stare as her eyes shifted to the pile of paperback romance novels on the floor. "Six months ago. 'Be Her Romance Hero.' I almost didn't want to share the secrets I learned while researching that one!"

Lacey held her hand in front of her mouth as she giggled. It all made perfect sense. "You freelance."

"Sure. The writer's pension plan. You'd be amazed how much companies will give away to a journalist, hoping he'll write a favorable comment about their product. Victoria's Secret just loved me!"

"I can imagine," she said as she accepted another magazine he held out, noticing the photos of lingerie-clad models interspersed with the text.

"You should see the stuff I got when I was doing the article on the adult toy industry."

She raised an eyebrow.

"It's shoved away in a box somewhere."

"Under your bed?"

"Hmm...that's possible," he said, a wicked glint in his eye. "Maybe I'll show you sometime."

A rush of naughty images skittered across Lacey's mind.

"So, are we clear? You are not trapped in Nate Logan's Sensual Passion Prison."

The laughter that had been building in Lacey

erupted across her lips. "I guess you know what I was imagining."

He nodded. "I have a pretty good idea."

"I didn't *immediately* go for the most obvious, damning explanation." She surprised herself with that realization.

"You would have a week ago."

She nodded. "Yes, I would, but not now." Lacey watched a look of pleasure cross his face. How much had she admitted with the small exchange? Did he realize she was growing to like and respect him? And was that a good thing, or a bad one?

"So how come you held onto this stuff?" she asked, taking a step back. "Couldn't you have given it to your sister?"

"I kept meaning to," Nate admitted. "She already took some of the lingerie, but Kelsey's a shrimpy little thing. Somehow I ended up with nightgowns meant for tall, curvy blondes."

Oh, boy. The teddy was singing to her from the hall closet.

"I've had most of the stuff in packing boxes in my storage unit since I moved here. Last week I heard about a new woman's shelter looking for donations, which is why I started digging stuff out and repacking it to give to them. The makeup, the books, magazines."

"The lingerie?"

"I decided to hold onto it." He leaned closer so he nearly whispered in her ear. "Who knows when a tall, curvy blonde needing a silk teddy might cross my path?"

She didn't breathe for twenty seconds. Nate, as if completely oblivious to her weak, shaky legs and over-heated face, turned away to answer the phone, which had just rung. Giving her an apologetic look, he sat at his desk and flipped the power switch for his computer. He appeared to be talking business.

As Nate spoke on the phone, Lacey knelt beside the pile of magazines he'd left on the floor. She began to straighten them, trying to be helpful, but one or two article titles on the covers caught her eye. Curious, she picked up a men's monthly from last year.

Glancing at Nate, she saw he was still engrossed in his conversation. She sat on the floor, leaned against the wall and opened the magazine. She scanned the table of contents until she found Nate's name, then turned to his article "Ten Ways to Make Up for Forgetting Her Birthday." Lacey chuckled as she read, noting Nate's witty writing voice.

Interested in reading more, she pulled out another magazine. This one had a feature Nate wrote about dealing with pesky kids. She chuckled when she read his suggestion that a clothes manufacturer start producing kid's coveralls made with Velcro with coordinating wallpaper, so people could stick the little beggars to the wall when they got too out of control.

He glanced over to see what she was doing. She held up the magazine and gave him a thumbs-up sign. He grinned and returned to his phone conversation.

The next magazine had another article by Nate. Once she read the first paragraph, Lacey wished she hadn't started it. It was titled "Lovemaking Secrets for the Everyday Stud," and was humorous, yes, but also deeply sensual and vivid. Throughout, several men discussed their tips on giving women pleasure. All Lacey could think about was that Nate had put these suggestions together, had blended them into one cohesive package. *How much did he learn? How much did he contribute?*

Lacey's breath came faster as she read the section on foreplay. When Nate commented that only a fool would rush through the rich, flavorful entrée to get to the quick dessert, she swallowed hard. The word pictures he drew mesmerized her. She continued to read, oblivious to everything except the seductive images his article evoked.

From his desk, Nate watched her. She hadn't noticed him finish his phone conversation. He studied her as she leaned against the wall, absorbed in the magazine. The late afternoon sunlight shone in through the window and caught the gold in her hair, making her heart-shaped face look like it was surrounded by a halo. Where some women were always conscious of their appearance, Lacey appeared completely at ease in her jeans and tank top. She wore no makeup, and her thick hair was coming loose from its braid. Her natural beauty still stunned him.

Nate saw a slow blush rise up her cheeks. Seeing her full lips part and her tongue dart out to moisten them, he took a deep breath. Judging by the rise and fall of her curvy breasts, she was doing some heavy breathing, too.

What the hell is she reading? Glancing at the cover of the magazine she held, he noted the date and remembered the issue. A smile curled across his lips as he watched Lacey Clark reading his views on lovemaking. He didn't doubt that was what she'd focused on. Then he started thinking about everything in the article. A lot of himself had gone into it, and he knew that had come across in the final piece.

His amusement faded as he watched her bite the corner of her lip and breathe deeper. She was fascinated by her reading, and Nate was fascinated by watching her. He could see the beat of her pulse in her throat, the way her hand tightened around the magazine. His gaze shifted to her body, and he saw her nipples tighten and grow hard against her clingy shirt.

Nate had never felt such a sudden rush of need. He swallowed hard, having a strong mental image of closing his mouth over her breast, sucking her taut nipple through the fabric of her top until she squirmed and begged him to remove the cotton obstacle.

She moved slightly, wiggling back a bit, as if her jeans were suddenly uncomfortable. Nate had to stifle a groan. Sitting a few feet away, watching her become physically aroused, was the sweetest torture he'd ever experienced.

When she finally finished reading, Lacey let out a ragged breath and closed the magazine, staring at the bulked-up male on its cover. But it was Nate's face she saw, his hard body she visualized. She had to swallow a few times as she remembered some of the techniques Nate had written about in the article she'd just read. She wished she had a glass of cold water. A big one. Better yet, an entire cold shower!

Gradually, hearing the ticking of a clock on Nate's desk and her own raging pulse, she recognized what she did *not* hear. Nate's voice. Almost afraid to look, she shifted her eyes to the left and slowly lifted her gaze. Nate still sat in the chair a few feet away. He wasn't, however, listening to his telephone conversation. Oh, no, that would have been too easy. Instead, the phone receiver rested in its cradle. Nate sat silently watching her, completely focused on what she was doing.

He didn't smile. No teasing light shone in his eyes. No boyish grin let her know he was amused by how engrossed she'd been in his article. Not that the word *engrossed* was exactly what she'd have chosen. *Turned on* would be more accurate. He obviously knew it. Because he wasn't smiling—he was smoldering. The expression on his face was pure need.

"Finished?" he asked. Lacey wondered how he managed to load so much meaning into a single word. No, she wasn't finished—nowhere near finished. But, oh, how she wanted to get started!

"Can you really do that? That thing with the feather?" She wondered where she'd found the nerve to voice her question.

The half smile on his lips and the slight narrowing of his eyes provided his answer. Yes, he obviously could.

She gulped. "The...kissing...the ten-minute kiss..."

He clenched his jaw, and she heard him let out a small groan. Finally he said, "You're killing me, Lacey."

She knew it. And she didn't care. Dropping the magazine, she rose to her knees and extended one arm to him in invitation, brushing the back of her hand across one hard, jeans-clad thigh. "Show me."

Nate didn't hesitate. Sliding off the chair, he knelt directly in front of her. They were close, face to face, almost chest to chest. He saw the cloudy look of passion in her blue eyes, though they hadn't yet touched. He understood it. His arousal matched hers, just from watching her, knowing what she was thinking, what she was imagining. Touching would be the icing on the cake.

"Show me *now*, Nate," she ordered with a moan when he did not move to take her in his arms. She slipped her hands up and laid them flat on his chest. Nate sucked in a breath as she slid them higher, until her fingers made contact with the bare skin of his neck. Her light touch on his flesh had him ready to explode.

He shook his head, encircling her wrists with his hands. Then he pulled her fingers away and pushed her hands to her sides. Tsking, he glanced over his shoulder at the clock. "Ten minutes. No touching. Just kissing."

Her eyes widened with anticipation as Nate finally leaned forward and touched his mouth to hers.

Slow. Soft. Very sweet. *Start gently*, he reminded himself, knowing the object of this particular erotic exercise was restraint. It was time to savor, time to focus on the pleasure of a kiss, to taste the sweetness of her tongue and test the sharp contours of her teeth. All the other delicious touching, stroking and caressing would come later. No question about it.

As he lost himself in the feel of her, in the taste of her, in her sweet scent, Nate came to a definite realization. *Ten minutes isn't going to be nearly enough.*

Lacey caught on quickly. She kept her hands at her sides, resisting the need to pull him closer, to bring his hard body against hers while they touched with only their mouths. At first the pressure was tremendous. Feeling a sob of pure need rise in the back of her throat, she thought she wouldn't really be able to go ten minutes without touching him, without pulling him down on top of her and touching all that smooth male skin. But she concentrated and thrust everything else out of her mind—everything except the sensations of the kiss they shared.

It was worth it. His lips played with hers, nibbling, stroking, soft then hard. When she licked at him, demanding more, he wouldn't accede to her demands, not until she was ready to scream in frustration. Then, finally, when she'd reached her boiling point, he gave her what she wanted. Opening his mouth, he caught her tongue in a sweet, hot dance that sent liquid fire running through her.

The kiss went on...and on...and on, until she no longer felt the touch just on her mouth. She could somehow feel it all over her body. She shook, felt weak and thought her knees were going to buckle beneath her. Unable to help it, she fell into him, needing his support. His arms were there to catch her, starting the pleasure building all over again.

Taking advantage of the moment, she wrapped her arms tightly around his neck and pulled his body hard against hers, tilting her head to kiss him more deeply. Pressing together from shoulder to knee, she could feel his need was as great as her own. His erection strained against his jeans, and she moaned, twisting against him, hearing by his ragged breathing that he was holding on by as thin a thread as she was.

Feeling his thick, hard breadth pressing right into the front of her jeans, she couldn't stand it anymore. She jerked against him, once, twice, finding from his rigid strength and the tight fabric of her jeans the release she'd craved from the minute she'd started reading the article.

And right there, fully clothed and without anything more than a kiss and an embrace, he made the earth move for her.

Nate had never seen anything more glorious in his life. Lacey seemed completely wild, uninhibited, lost in sensation. He loved that he made her eyes grow wide, that she looked without fully seeing. Her cries rang sweetly in his ears, and he watched as her head fell back when she reached her peak.

He nearly followed her. It took all his control not to let her cry of pleasure bring him over the edge, too. Somehow, maybe by focusing on the emotions darting around in his head as he watched her, he managed to avoid climaxing, too.

Still holding her, sated and replete in his arms, he lowered her to the floor. She didn't even open her eyes as he stretched out next to her. Nate remained silent, watching the expressions crossing Lacey's beautiful face. Her quickened breath gradually slowed, and the high color in her cheeks receded.

Finally, she opened her eyes and looked at him. "Nathan?"

"Yes, Lacey?"

"I think you'd better give me a few minutes before you get the feather."

A MOMENT LATER, when Lacey's pulse finally returned to normal and she had a chance to think about what had just happened, she slowly sat up. Nate sat beside her, his elbow resting on one upraised knee, a tender look in his eyes. Lacey didn't know what to say. What did one say at a time like this? *Uh, thanks for the orgasm—is it time to eat?*

"You okay?" he finally asked.

She nodded, then whispered, "I didn't plan this."

"I know."

She knew she had to be honest. "I won't lie and say my brain had nothing to do with it. My brain is engaged enough to know that as much as I wanted this, it's simply impossible."

"Nah. Unlikely, maybe. Unexpected, yeah. Not impossible."

Lacey rose to her feet, holding her arms tightly across her chest. "Nate, aside from the fact that I don't do casual relationships, you and I are working together. How are we going to be able to handle the story if we..."

He rose, too. "Whoa, whoa, back up a second. What makes you think there's anything casual about this?"

"Oh, come on, this has been about one thing since the minute we met."

His eyes narrowed. "Yeah, what's that one thing?"

She looked at her hands and mumbled, "Well, sex, of course. Physical attraction."

He was silent for a moment, and when she glanced at him, she saw a slight tightening of his jaw. "Just sex?"

"Well, isn't it?" Even as she said the words, she knew it *wasn't* all, not on her part! Dammit, it *wasn't* just about sex, because Lacey wasn't the type of person who could separate sex from emotion. It was all wrapped up in one package for her.

She couldn't tell him that, though. Couldn't admit her emotions were already engaged, that she liked him, thought about him constantly, visualized his response to things she did or said throughout her day. Because her relationship with Nate wasn't about emotions. It was about laughter and attraction, flirtation and seduction.

Not emotion. Not commitment. Not soul mates or split aparts or happily ever afters with couples who liked each other as much as they loved each other. He wouldn't understand her needs, certainly wouldn't appreciate her feelings. In the end she'd look like a romantic fool, and he'd feel guilty, miserable and embarrassed. Too many times she'd seen her father's reaction to girlfriends who'd wanted more than he was able to give for her to want to see it coming from Nate.

Finally, Nate muttered a curse. Shaking his head, he turned to leave the room. "I gotta check the sauce."

After he'd left, Lacey ran a weary hand over her brow. Should she have said something? Told him the truth? That she wanted him so much he filled her dreams at night? That she liked him? Admired the fond way he talked about his sister, thought he was a hell of a writer and appreciated his kindness when she'd been spilling her guts earlier? Did he need to know she'd adored the way they'd made love on the trampoline, applauded the way he'd manipulated her father and almost loved him for not taking what she'd silently offered in her kitchen the other morning?

No. He didn't need to know any of those things. He wouldn't *want* to know any of these things. So he was annoyed now. Better that than if she'd admitted the truth and had to watch him backpedal to get away from the sappy girl who really believed the mushy stuff she wrote about in her columns.

"But I do," she murmured. "I do." She spoke forcefully, pushing Nate's swivel chair out of her way in frustration. The chair hit the corner of the desk, knocking against a small microcassette tape recorder that had been sitting on it. The recorder fell to the floor, but not before the play button struck the arm of the chair and was depressed.

A moment later she heard Nate's voice filling the room. Nate's voice...talking about her.

8

NATE DIDN'T JUST chop the celery for the salad, he damn near puréed it. Then he went to work on the green pepper. Hacking the vegetables kept him from going in the office and telling Lacey Clark exactly what he thought.

"Nothing but sex," he muttered in disgust.

A comment like that might have been dead-on a few years ago, when he'd been younger, played the field more. Now, it was way off base. What was going on between him and Lacey involved a lot more than just sex.

Why he was so angry, he really couldn't say. It wasn't like they'd dated for months. He was fully aware they'd only met a week ago. So why did he feel so certain they were meant to be together? More important, why did she *not* feel that way?

Their conversation had revealed a lot of things about the woman—like why she fought so hard against that irrepressible spark in her personality. She'd assumed the responsibility for the well-being of her mother's marriage at the age of twelve. As if that weren't enough, she'd taken on a parental role with her real father.

They all needed different things from her. And she tried to please them all. Which meant never pleasing herself.

"You need to please yourself, Lacey," he said as he

dropped the knife on the cutting board and leaned against the counter.

"I know I do."

Surprised at the sound of her voice, Nate turned suddenly and saw her standing in the arched opening between the kitchen and living room.

Then Nate's heart stopped. Hell, the entire world might have stopped for all he knew. He was completely unable to breathe as he saw her there, backlit by the sun pouring in from the living room windows.

The light made her glow.

She made him burn.

She wore the purple teddy that had been hanging in his hall closet for months. The lingerie looked like it had been created for her. It fit perfectly, from the tiny spaghetti straps resting on her shoulders to the bit of silk and lace barely covering her breasts. It curved in at the waist and cut high on her hips, coming down to a narrow dark strip caught between her thighs. The outfit revealed more than it covered. Nate went weak-kneed. It was a damn good thing he was leaning against the counter.

Her blond hair curled loosely around her face. Her lips were pouty and full, her eyes...oh, her blue eyes...there was mystery in those depths. Mystery and desire and need.

"I need to please myself, Nate," she repeated. "And you, I think, are what I need to do that."

He almost reached for her. Then he stopped. He *forced* himself to stop. "Why? Why now?"

His own voice answered him. Confused, it took him a moment to realize Lacey was holding the new micro-cassette recorder he'd bought the day before to replace the one he'd ruined in the pool. He suddenly remembered exactly what he'd said while testing it the night before. He'd been lying in his bed late in the night, thinking about her, fantasizing about her, knowing he'd dream of her, wanting her so bad it made him shake. His voice now revealed every bit of that.

"What do women want? What do *you* want is the real question. How can a woman I barely know make me so crazy I can't sleep, can't think, can't work? You did it, Lacey. You've tapped into a part of me I didn't even know existed. How the hell I walked away from you Tuesday is beyond me."

Nate didn't move an inch as they both listened to his raging need for her. She remained just as still, watching him, waiting for his reaction to his own unthinking, late-night confession.

"Didn't you feel it? What a stupid question—of course you did. I watched your face as you felt every sensation, and all I could think was how beautiful you were. How much I wanted to be inside you, feeling you tighten around me at the moment you went over the edge. I wanted to fly off that cliff with you."

Heat rushed through Nate, his words sending sparks shooting through his body to settle with hot, pounding insistence at his sex. He got hard for her without a single touch, not even a kiss. She was standing across the damn room, but watching her listen to his voice—talking about what he wanted to do to her—made him hotter than he'd ever felt before.

She was apparently having the same reaction. Even from here he saw the color rise in her cheeks. Her mouth opened as she sucked in deeper breaths.

"All I could think about," the voice continued, "was laying you back on that table, naked, hungry. I wanted to bend down and feast on you, see if you tasted as sweet as you smelled. Put my mouth on you and make you scream. And then become part of you, bury myself deep inside you, let you take over my body the way you've taken over my brain since the minute we met."

"Oh," Lacey gasped, reaching for the back of a kitchen chair for support. "I didn't listen this far."

"Over and over again, Lacey. I want to know you inside and out, to brand myself on you so you'll feel the same insane need whenever you hear my name. To drive every other man in the world out of your realm of existence until you think of nothing but me. Of us. Hot, wet, sweaty, hard and frantic. Or sweet and slow. God knows I want you every way it's possible to have you."

She clicked off the tape. A long, heavy moment of silence hung in the air of the kitchen as the two of them stared at each other. She, looking dazed, sensuous, aroused. He, feeling the same—plus exposed and more open than he'd ever felt in his life.

Yet he also wondered what this meant. Her. Dressed like that. Looking at him like she wanted to eat him up.

"What's changed in the past ten minutes?" he finally asked, staying right where he was. If he took a step toward her he was going to be gone. Just *gone*. Until at least tomorrow. Or Monday. For the next twenty years. Or for a lifetime.

"It's not one-sided," she finally replied with shaky certainty. "There's nothing *casual* about this. I understand that now. Whatever this is between us, Nathan, I want to go further. I want more. For as long as I can have it. As much as you're willing to give."

Her eyes shifted down, her stare devouring him, darkening as she saw his obvious reaction to her in the uncomfortable tightness of his jeans. Yeah, he had a *lot* to give her.

Then he moved. A slow smile spread across his lips, a smile he knew was full of promise and anticipation, desire and excitement.

"Nate..."

"No more words, Lacey."

When he reached her side, she gasped as he bent and picked her up in his arms. He didn't hesitate, simply turned and carried her out of the kitchen and down the short hall of his apartment. To his bedroom.

"I've pictured you here," he said as he lowered her to his king-size bed. Nate liked how she looked there, noting the way she curled and arched sinuously against the soft fabric beneath her nearly naked body.

"I've pictured you in many places," she admitted with a deep, erotic sigh.

"Here?" he asked, just before he took her mouth in a hot, insistent kiss, catching her tongue with his and tasting her thoroughly.

"Yes," she whispered when their mouths broke apart.

He lowered his head to her neck, sucking and nibbling his way down to her tender nape. "Here?"

She shifted, lifting her body, whimpering. "Yes," she finally managed to say.

Nate moved lower, to the curve of one creamy breast, breathing through the silk fabric of the teddy until she squirmed. "And here?" he asked. Only after she nodded mindlessly did he open his mouth on her, slipping his tongue beneath the lace to lick at her sweetly puckered nipple.

"Nate!" she cried, wrapping her hands in his hair as he thoroughly lathed and sucked her sensitive flesh.

"Not right? You want something else?" he whispered before moving to pay attention to her other breast.

"I want everything else," she admitted hoarsely.

"So do I." Then he lowered his head, sampling more.

Lacey quite simply lost her mind when he moved his mouth down her belly, breathing hotly over the slick fabric of the teddy. She was incoherent, one living, writhing, erotic being in need of his kiss, his touch, his mouth. She twisted against him and almost screamed when he finally moved to the juncture of her thighs.

He unsnapped the teddy with his teeth.

"I can't believe this," she muttered as she felt the waves of pleasure washing over her and knew she was close to climaxing. "You make me come in my sleep."

He chuckled throatily. "Ditto."

When he nudged the damp silk away from her flesh and moved his mouth over her, tasting her with flicks of his sweet, hot tongue, she really did scream. And then she flew apart in a completely shattering orgasm. Her second of the afternoon.

He caught her scream with a kiss that stole her breath and built the pleasure all over again. Nate's tongue plunged deep into her mouth, and Lacey met each thrust, pushing back with her own in a duel to determine who was more aroused. She figured it was a draw. His thick erection pressed ravenously against his jeans, pulsing against her naked, exposed sex. Her body jerked against him instinctively. He groaned from deep in his throat as she slid one leg around his hips and pulled him tightly against her, rubbing herself against his strength, silently urging him to strip off his clothes and just *take* her.

When he lifted his mouth from hers only to scrape kisses along her jaw, to her neck and earlobe, Lacey whimpered.

"You know what I want," Nate whispered heavily. "You heard it right from my own mouth on that tape. Now what is it *you* want?"

She shivered, closed her eyes, picturing what she wanted to do with this man. Everything. Anything. Once, and then over and over again. "I want you to say it again. I want to hear every little thing you plan to do to me," she finally managed to gasp. "And then I want you to *do* it."

As he knelt beside her and shrugged off his jeans and shirt, he chuckled. The throaty, warm sound tantalized her almost as much as the sight of his perfect naked form. She watched the play of muscles beneath his skin, feeling intensely feminine as she studied the differences in their bodies. When she saw the power of his desire for her, that thick, throbbing erection, she whimpered, remembering how he'd filled her up last Friday, all the way to the depths of her being. She wanted that again. She was ready for it. She'd been waiting for him for a long, long time—since before she even knew Nate Logan existed.

"I plan to do everything to you...with you," he whispered as he gently slipped the teddy over her head, tossing it to the floor with his clothes. "But, first, I want to see you."

His eyes darkened as he stared at her. Lacey liked his stare, liked the hot appreciation in his eyes. She made no effort to move away or to cover herself. She was beautiful to him, and she knew it. As beautiful to him as he was to her.

"Lovely," he murmured as he looked at her.

He gazed his fill, the intensity in his eyes as potent as a touch, but not enough...not nearly enough. When she reached up, he caught her hands, raised them above her head and held them out of the way. She was nearly sobbing by the time he bent lower and licked the tip of her breast in one long, wet caress. Before she could cry out, he covered her with his mouth, sucking, stroking, even biting lightly as she squirmed beneath him.

"I can't seem to stop touching you," he muttered, releasing her hands so he could use his own to tease and cajole her other aching nipple. He went back and forth, using tongue, teeth and lips, until Lacey was sure she couldn't take it.

"Please," she whispered, twisting beneath him.

Leaning forward, Lacey reached out to run her hands across his chest, curling her fingers in the hair that trailed a line across his rippling stomach. His harsh breaths, the slight tremor in his hand as he reached out to catch her hip, told her how much he wanted her.

She couldn't resist reaching for his sex, taking that silky-steel warmth into her palm. He jerked hard when she closed her fingers around his erection, sliding her hand down in a long, smooth stroke as unhurried as it was deliberate. She squeezed lightly and was rewarded by his low groan of satisfaction.

"I don't think I could ever get tired of looking at you, touching you," he informed her, his voice husky and thick, "or having you touch me."

"Oh, Nate," she breathed, wondering how she could ever withstand more of this never-ending pleasure.

Finally he touched her lower, testing the slickness

he'd created. His fingers slid easily into her, joining in the rhythm of the slow movement of his tongue in her mouth, of her hand on him, sliding up and down in smooth, delicious strokes.

He pulled away only long enough to grab a condom from a bedside table drawer. She watched him sheathe himself. Then he was back, touching her, stroking her, using his fingertips to draw her so close to that shattering peak once again.

This time, she decided, he wasn't going to push her over the edge without being fully inside her when he made it happen. The man's control was phenomenal, but she wanted it gone. She wanted him out of control, as insane and insatiable as she was.

"Now, Nate," she said, a husky note in her voice, "let me tell you what *I* want."

He pressed kisses on her throat, holding himself out of reach, still testing his control and hers. "Tell me, Lacey. Tell me what you want. Anything."

"I want you to..." She leaned close to his ear, feeling bold, feeling like someone else, someone sensual and strong and very, very naughty. Then she whispered the last few words and felt his control snap. He grabbed her hips, pulled her forward and thrust into her in one long, hard stroke.

"Yes," she said with a pleasure-filled gasp, thrilled her words had inflamed him. "That's exactly what I want."

He remained unmoving deep inside her and she felt the throbbing of his erection. Before him, it had been a long time for her, a long time since she'd made love. Actually, compared to this, she didn't think she'd ever *really* made love. As impossible as it seemed given their differences, the way they'd met, she felt sure she was falling in love with Nate Logan.

It was perfect. He was perfect. Thick and heavy, hot and deep. She lay still, savoring the feel of him buried to the hilt. Squeezing him inside her, she heard him hiss as he felt the pulsing caresses within her body.

"You were made for me," he whispered as he began to move.

His every movement was deliberate. He stroked her slowly, drawing his body almost completely out of hers and sliding back while she whimpered in delight. Then pulling out again only to plunge, hard, fast, unexpected, making her scream. Finally, after what seemed to be hours of sensual torment, he seemed to lose control. He held tightly to her hips, driving into her again and again until Lacey began to feel weak. She dropped her head back, arching herself higher, wanting him even closer. As if sensing her need, he slid his arm under her leg and drew it up over his shoulder.

The pleasure was intense. Mind-numbing. Scream-inducing. As he drove ever deeper into her, she had to clutch tightly to his shoulders, holding on as he took her higher and higher, beyond anything she'd ever felt, any pleasure she'd ever imagined.

"You're not flying alone this time, Lacey," he muttered.

She watched his body tense, his face tighten, and Lacey pulled his mouth down to hers. As they kissed in a wet, sweet mating of lips and tongues, she heard him moan, felt him shudder. Lacey gave herself over to sensation, wanting to reach her climax with him. As if connected mentally as well as physically, they both opened their eyes wide, staring deeply at each other as they reached that cliff and, together, flew off.

THEY EVENTUALLY left the bed—after a few hours and another seriously intense round of lovemaking. Lacey wondered if she'd be able to stand on her legs, so shaky and weak they were. She felt lethargic, happy and fulfilled.

Nate was an incredible lover. She'd truly never imagined her body capable of such physical pleasure. Not until he'd shown her. Spent *hours* showing her.

He seemed to delight in touching her, kissing her endlessly. If she hadn't read his article on lovemaking, she might have been surprised by his utter delight in caressing every inch of her, in bringing her to the edge over and over again, not driving into her until they were both in a complete frenzy.

The orgasms were shocking. Raw and powerful. Even more intense was the emotional connection Lacey felt when his body was joined with hers. Such intimacy left her feeling tender and vulnerable, maddeningly aroused and somewhat overwhelmed all at the same time.

Finally, sometime after eight, hunger forced them out of bed and they went into the kitchen together. Nate wore only a pair of boxer shorts, Lacey the purple silk robe.

"Has the sauce completely evaporated?" she asked as Nate opened the pot on the stove.

"Nah. Simmering for hours is the secret." He stirred the pot and put on some water for spaghetti.

"Guess it's lucky we found something to do to occupy our time while it simmered."

They ate by candlelight at the coffee table in the living room. Sitting on the floor, facing each other across the table, they laughed and talked, exchanging sips of wine and bites of pasta. Lacey found it amazing that they were so comfortable and at ease with one another. On a few occasions, she caught Nate staring at her with a wickedly reminiscent expression on his face and knew he was remembering something delicious they'd done together in his bed. She shivered, knowing without asking that there would be more to come before the night ended.

Finally, after a leisurely meal, Nate rose to clean up. "Stay here, have another glass of wine. I'll take care of this."

"You'll spoil me," she said with a lazy smile as he cleared away their dishes. "That was delicious. You really can cook."

"You might be surprised by some of the things I can do."

She lowered her eyes flirtatiously. "I don't know. I've seen firsthand some of the things you're capable of, though, I seem to recall something in that article about…"

"Yes?"

"A juicy red strawberry?"

His eyes darkened, and a confident smile creased his face. "I think I have some in the fridge."

Lacey shivered as she watched him walk out of the room, carrying the dishes. She'd never known it was possible to be so creative with fruit until she'd read the shockingly arousing suggestion in his article earlier that day. She also still wanted to experience the feather firsthand.

Reaching toward the stereo, which stood under the front window, Lacey turned up the volume on the radio. She sipped her wine, listening to the low, soothing notes of a bluesy song. As the song ended, a prerecorded musical introduction came on. Lacey recognized the lead-in to a wildly popular call-in show.

"Perfect," she mused aloud.

Then a sultry woman's voice emerged from the speakers. "Good evening, Baltimore, this is Lady Love. And tonight, I'm feeling a just a little bit naughty."

Lacey stretched lazily. *That makes two of us.*

"Have you ever gotten a thrill at the thought of doing something especially erotic?" the radio deejay continued. "Been tempted to go beyond your normal boundaries and explore? Push the envelope?"

Well, yes, actually, a few hours ago.

"We all know passion and desire are an integral part of any serious relationship. But how far are you willing to go with your lover? How much would you trust him when it comes to, shall we say, experimenting?" The voice paused for a few suggestive seconds.

A rush of visual images flooded Lacey's mind. She trusted Nate completely, at least in the bedroom.

"Eroticism. Pushing the envelope. Sensual risks. That's our topic tonight on 'Night Whispers.'"

She wished he'd hurry up in the kitchen. She had a feeling this might be the type of program that would be fun to listen to with someone else—like a lover. It amazed her to think she now actually *had* a lover.

"How far would you go?" Lady Love continued. "Does eroticism have a place in a healthy adult relationship? Don't go away now. We've got a lot to talk about. My producer, Brian, tells me we're going to have to use a longer-than-usual time delay tonight with your calls. We wouldn't want anyone getting too carried away. But this is 'Night Whispers'...so let's take it to the edge, shall we?"

Picking up a magazine from beneath the coffee table,

Lacey used it to fan her suddenly overheated face during the commercial break. She leaned back, resting her head on the seat of the couch, feeling outside herself as she acknowledged just how interesting she'd found the deejay's comments. They made her think of going even farther with Nate. She'd already gone way beyond what she'd ever experienced with anyone else. But she still wanted more. Lacey felt completely free, self-indulgent and very much in tune with her senses, not to mention her sexuality.

She wanted to explore the possibilities.

Lifting her head, she opened her eyes and studied the deep crimson shade of the wine as she brought her glass to her lips. Sipping from it, she sighed as liquid warmth filled her mouth. The silk robe wisped against her body with delightful friction. Lacey shifted her shoulders, liking the feel of the fabric against her skin. Her nipples hardened in response, suddenly tender and incredibly sensitive.

Lacey bent her leg, lifting one knee and dropping her arm over it in relaxation. Her other limb remained on the floor, loose and pliant, and Lacey felt cool air on her inner thighs as the robe parted.

She wore nothing beneath.

No mental voice of modesty screamed at her to tug the robe closed, to cover herself. Part of her shivered in anticipation at the thought of Nate walking into the room and seeing her like this. Exposed. Inviting. Ready for more.

She breathed deeply, still tasting the wine on her tongue, catching a hint of vanilla scent from the candle flickering on the table. She also noted the earthier essence of hot passion she and Nate had created earlier, and her body's renewed arousal.

As the voice on the radio returned, Lacey recognized the utter sensuality of the moment. She reveled in it.

"Welcome back, Baltimore, this is Lady Love, and tonight we're talking about eroticism. As with many of the topics we discuss here on 'Night Whispers,' the word erotic can mean different things to different people. I know one woman who says the most erotic evening she ever spent started when her husband decided to paint her toenails."

Lacey thought about that. Having Nate do something so simple but so intimate…touching her sensitive feet with those hands. Yes, she could definitely see the erotic possibilities there.

"Erotic pleasures, when explored by two people who truly care about each other, can add a great deal to a sensual relationship. The key is trust, and a willingness to go just a bit further."

Exactly what Lacey had been thinking. She trusted. She was willing.

"Ladies, if you know he cares about you, if you know he'd never hurt you, how far would you go? Gentle restraints? Unusual locations for lovemaking— where there's perhaps the risk of exposure?" She paused. "Special little toys?"

Lacey sucked in a deep breath, remembering Nate's comment about sex toys. She'd never even *seen* one. Nor would she know what to do with one if she did!

He could show me.

A whimper escaped her lips. She shifted, allowing the robe to slip off her shoulder until it barely covered the puckered nipple of one breast.

"Gentlemen, what do you find most erotic about a woman? Is it the way she moves? The way she whispers or screams out her pleasure? Is it the wicked joy in her eyes as she lets you take her somewhere you've never gone before? The trust she places in you when she allows you to indulge her every sensual desire?"

Lacey breathed deeply, affected by the sensory input surrounding her—the heady wine, the slick silk, the flickering candlelight—and the mental images the radio deejay evoked. Her hand moved over the robe, lightly brushing the curve of her breast before dropping to her thigh.

"What's your erotic fantasy?" the deejay continued. "Ladies, if he wants to play, wants you as his concubine for the night, will you let him make you his love slave?"

"Yes," Lacey whispered, unable to help herself.

"And you men, if your woman touches herself," the deejay continued, "indulging in the joys of her own body, do you shake in anticipation?"

Lacey unclenched the hand on her leg, brushing her fingers high on her inner thigh.

"Oh, God, yes."

She hadn't spoken. Nate's deep, male voice had uttered the hoarse words.

Lacey didn't move, didn't start with surprise. She'd known he'd come back soon, known he'd find her waiting.

He stood a few feet away, watching her. At the sight of the powerful erection beneath his silk boxers, she sighed with pleasure. "Do you listen to this show?"

Not answering, he walked over and turned the radio off, then gave her his full attention.

"You don't listen to 'Night Whispers'?"

He shook his head slowly. "I'd much rather hear *you* say the words, Lacey."

She played coy, her hand still resting in her lap, her

robe still dangling precariously off her shoulder. "Which words would those be?"

He didn't move. Just stared at her from above. Lacey lowered her voice, remembering the seductiveness of the deejay's whisper. "What's your erotic fantasy, Nate?" She watched him draw in a deep breath. "What do you find most sensual about a woman?"

This time he answered, his eyes glittering in the candlelight. "The curve of your lips. The way your hair falls over your cheek. The way you whimper when I kiss the back of your knee."

It was her turn to breathe deeply.

"The way your eyes grow wide and you gasp when I'm deep inside you."

Lacey had never before realized the seductive power of whispered fantasies. She did now.

"The way you taste."

She had to close her eyes briefly. But she wasn't to be outdone. Remembering more of the deejay's words, she said, "How far would you go?" She knew her voice held a note of challenge. "If she touches herself, do you shake in anticipation?"

He stepped closer, lowering his eyes to gaze at her lap, where her fingers rested lightly on her thigh. His mouth opened, and she saw the effort it took for him to draw in a choppy breath. "I can't imagine anything I'd rather see right now," he finally replied.

The heat in his stare made her want to go on. The tenderness in his smile gave her the courage to do exactly that.

She parted her thighs a bit more, hearing him groan in response as he looked his fill. Uncertain but wanting very badly to push him to the limits of his control as he'd done to her earlier, she slipped her fingers into the curls between her legs.

Nate felt the world tilt and nearly fell to the floor. "You're glorious," he somehow managed to mutter. He struggled to pull the thick, hot air of the room into his mouth. "You leave me breathless."

A sultry smile, full of womanly power and mystery, crossed her lips. Nate didn't think he'd ever seen Lacey looking quite that way—free and sensual, confident and seductive.

He'd never imagined the eroticism of seeing a woman's hands on her own body. This woman. This body. The moment became more powerful with the realization that this was *Lacey*, who'd tried so hard to hide this provocative part of herself. This was *his* Lacey, the real, uninhibited woman, slipping her fingers across the wet folds of her flesh, dropping her head back and moaning across parted lips as she gave herself pleasure.

If he'd been a man with less control over his responses, he would have exploded right then and there. He wanted her desperately. In every way possible. Tonight. For a lifetime.

First, however, he wanted to watch her come to life, watch the walls she'd so carefully constructed around herself come tumbling down one by one as she gave in to her true nature.

As a flush rose in her cheeks and the robe fell further down her arms to bare one pale breast, he couldn't resist kneeling beside her. She immediately opened her eyes, smiling at him.

"Please don't stop on my account," he murmured. "Pretend I'm not even here." Leaning forward, he bent to nibble on the curve of her breast, cupping the fullness in his hand. She sighed, arching back, silently telling him what she wanted.

He took his time giving it to her. Nate stroked and caressed her fully before finally moving his lips over her nipple and sucking it into his mouth. Her tiny sounds inflamed him; the sweet rose and musky scent of her made him lose his mind.

As he suckled her, she hissed, bringing one hand up to tangle in his hair. When he turned his attention to her other breast, nudging the robe completely off, she arched higher, sliding up until she half-reclined on the couch. Then both her hands were tangling in his hair, holding him close to her chest.

He pulled one hand free, catching it in his own. Bringing her fingers to his lips, he sucked one into his mouth, tasting her, loving the taste of her.

"I want..."

"What, Lacey?" he murmured as he returned his attention to her neck, her earlobe and the smooth flesh of her shoulder.

"I want *your* hands on me now."

He shook his head. "Sorry. I want my *mouth* on you now," he replied as he lifted her until she reclined on the couch.

She cried out when he lowered his head and lapped at her damp curls. He didn't relent, caressing her, sliding his fingers into her body as well as using his lips and tongue to bring her to a writhing frenzy on the couch. Only when she screamed out in completion did he pick her up and carry her to his bedroom.

"Not here," she said as he lowered her to stand next to him. Her face was still rosy and flushed from her recent orgasm. Nate reached for a condom from the bedside table. Not sure what she wanted, but more than willing to follow her lead, he watched her walk toward the door, naked, clothed only in the moonlight shining through the windows of his room.

She paused in the doorway, giving him a come-hither stare over one bare shoulder. "I've been fantasizing about your weight bench since the minute I saw it."

He chuckled in anticipation, suddenly seeing the myriad possibilities. She already had something in mind, it appeared, because as soon as he entered his office, she pointed to the bench. "Lie down. Hold onto the bars as if your hands are tied to it. This time I'm in control."

He liked this new side of her. This possessive, demanding side, and the wickedness in her blue eyes. Doing as she asked, he lay back, his arms over his head, holding the empty cradles where the weight bar would normally rest. "Like this?"

She nodded, then, with slow, deliberate strokes, ran her hands down his bare torso to the waistband of his boxers.

He reached for her.

"Ah, ah. Do I really have to tie you up?" she scolded.

The thought was shocking. Provocative. Enticing. "I'll be good," he finally replied wistfully.

"Oh, there's no question about that, Nate Logan. No question at all."

He chuckled at her vehemence.

"You're the love slave. And you're ordered to stay very still. I'm going to give you a taste of your own medicine, Mr. Everyday Stud."

Smiling as he recognized the title of his article, Nate knew he was in for a long night of sensual torment. "Turnabout is fair play," he murmured, knowing how much he'd enjoyed holding back, giving her pleasure while waiting for his own until he couldn't stand it anymore. Who was he to argue if she wanted the same?

"I never imagined how much I'd like to play," Lacey replied as she finally moved her fingers below the elastic waistband and eased the boxers off his body.

And play she did. Until it was Nate who begged for mercy. Only after he threatened serious retaliation did she move her mouth off him and straddle him on the bench. She took delight in teasing him as she slipped a condom over his erection, taking her sweet time until he gritted his teeth and groaned in frustration. Then, finally, she engulfed him with her wet heat in one long, smooth stroke.

"Oh, I like this bench, Nate," she whispered throatily. "This might just be my favorite spot in your home."

"Wait'll you see my bathtub," he managed to mutter.

Then she began to move, retaining control, setting the pace for their pleasure. He let her, keeping his hands on the bars, focusing on the slide of his skin against hers as she moved her body up and down.

As Lacey, naked, glorious, confident and in control, reached her climax, crying out her delight, Nate realized something.

He simply wasn't going to let her go.

9

WHEN SHE WOKE the next morning, Lacey realized within five seconds that she wasn't in her own bed. The jewel-toned sheets, so unlike her lemon-yellow ones, provided the first clue. There was also the heavy, masculine arm draped across her hip. Not to mention the hard, muscular thigh entwined with her legs.

She glanced at Nate, who slept on his side facing her. Even now, his lips were curled into a tiny smile. He appeared to be having a very nice dream.

Or maybe he was remembering.

"Oh, boy," she whispered at the thought of everything they'd done together during the long hours of the previous night. When she paused to consider, though, she felt no regret. Yes, she'd had a recklessly erotic encounter with a man she'd only known a week, but she'd done nothing of which she was ashamed. They were both single, unattached and wildly attracted to one another. If her feelings went even deeper, if she suspected she might be on the verge of falling head over heels in love with him—well, she hadn't been stupid enough to let him know that, had she? She hadn't made declarations, hadn't demanded promises. She'd indulged her body and protected her heart. Both on the most magnificent night of her life.

Lacey eased out of bed, made her way into the bathroom and took a long shower. As she washed, every touch on her skin brought back the feel of Nate's hands, his lips. She leaned her head against the cool tile of the shower wall, letting the water pelt her, trying to ease muscles that were sore from last night's more frenzied activity. The mental images brought heat to her cheeks.

Though she knew she should be embarrassed down to her toes, particularly when remembering how she'd reacted to the radio show, Lacey felt no humiliation. A week ago she hadn't had the confidence to touch herself so intimately, even in private. Now, thanks to Nate, she could finally face her deep sensual needs. Before, she'd hidden them, repressed them, only allowing herself silly luxuries like expensive underclothes. No more. Whatever happened between her and Nate now, she wouldn't hide that aspect of herself any longer.

When Lacey emerged from the bathroom, wrapped in a towel, she found the bedroom empty. Not quite as bold as she'd been the night before, she pulled on her clothes before she went looking for Nate. She followed the sound of clanging dishes to his kitchen.

"Good morning," she said softly as she found him scrambling eggs at the stove. He'd pulled on a pair of jeans, too. "I hope I didn't wake you."

Nate turned and gave her a cheerful smile. "Good morning to you. I woke as soon as I felt you get up. I almost joined you in the shower."

Her heart picked up its pace. "What stopped you?"

"I figured you might need a little time alone this morning," he said, his expression tender.

He was right. Lacey appreciated his consideration. Though a morning shower together *did* sound enticing...

"So instead of seducing you into spending the day with me," he continued, "I decided I'd appeal to your stomach. You are hungry, right?"

She nodded. "Breakfast would be great, thanks. Then I really should get home."

"Why? I'd hoped we could do something together today. Go to the harbor, or maybe drive down to Annapolis."

Though she was tempted, Lacey realized that she did need some time alone—to think and absorb what had happened in the past twenty-four hours. She needed to figure out what had changed in her physical relationship with Nate and in her views of herself and her world. She'd woken up feeling like a different person today. She needed to get to know herself again.

"I don't think so," she finally replied. "I have things to do. And I'm sure you do, too."

"We could call it research," Nate said, a cajoling tone in his voice. "We'll interview some midshipmen for the story."

Lacey grinned. "Middies in dress whites. Now you're talking."

He pointed the spatula toward her. "Uh-uh. No drooling over muscle-bound meatheads on our first date."

"Date? You're asking me on a date?"

He gave her an offended look, but she saw the humor in his eyes. "Oh, so I'm good enough to sleep with, but not good enough to date?"

"I think we skipped right past the dating chapter in the manual," she retorted dryly.

"I think we could rewrite that manual, Lacey." He chuckled. "Though, yes, I suppose it's customary to go on the first date before getting wild on the living room floor. Or the weight bench. Or the bed."

"Don't forget the trampoline," she managed to say with a saucy grin, "and my kitchen table."

"How about a private skybox at Camden Yards?" he said.

She raised an inquisitive eyebrow. "Did I forget something?"

He shook his head and sighed. "My fantasy. You and me in a private skybox, giving new meaning to the seventh-inning stretch."

Some devil made her reply, "J.T. has a skybox."

"When's the Orioles' next home game?"

"I have no idea," she replied, chuckling at his enthusiasm. "Besides, those skyboxes aren't completely private."

A wicked expression crossed his face as he fantasized aloud. "We could be discreet." He lowered his voice. "I think I've got something hanging in the closet that you could wear under a sexy little miniskirt. Lacy and black. And *very* accessible."

She gulped, remembering a wicked ensemble she'd spotted in the hall closet the day before. Something with unusually placed zippers. And slits. "I don't own a sexy little miniskirt," she finally managed to whisper.

"I'll buy you one. Flirty and red. You could sit on my lap and no one would ever realize I had my hands on you. No one would see me touching you or know I was sliding into you. That is, unless you couldn't help yourself and screamed when I made you come right then and there amid thousands of people."

"You're bluffing," she said breathlessly, getting caught up in the images he evoked. "You wouldn't dare."

"Ask your father for a game schedule," he cajoled, "and I'll show you what I'd dare."

His eyes held both a promise and a challenge. Though she shook her head reprovingly, Lacey knew darn well she'd end up asking her father for the schedule. Just out of curiosity.

"Okay, wicked man," she finally said with a firm shake of her head, "feed me. All this fantasizing is making me hungry."

"Fantasizing is supposed to make you hungry," he said as he turned his attention to the stove.

"I mean hungry for food." Seeing their breakfast was nearly ready, Lacey gathered some dishes and set the small kitchen table. "I assume we're eating in here this morning?"

"I dunno, I think I liked feasting in the living room last night."

She felt a blush rush into her cheeks again. Yes, he'd definitely feasted—on her.

After placing breakfast on the table, Nate sat opposite her.

"Where'd you learn to cook?" Lacey asked after sampling her eggs. "I can barely manage toast."

"My mother believed in making everyone in the family self-sufficient. We used to have to take turns cooking. Of course, my sister, Kelsey, usually found a way to get out of it on her nights. She could talk her way out of anything." An amused expression crossed his face.

"What?"

"I never thought that one day I'd be so thankful she's got such a big mouth."

She didn't understand. "What do you mean?"

"You remember when you asked me last night if I listen to 'Night Whispers'?"

She nodded. "You said you didn't, which kind of surprised me. I thought every guy in Baltimore was nuts about Lady Love."

Nate snorted. "Not exactly."

"Why not? Those sexy topics, the sultry voice. And I've heard she's gorgeous."

"Well, whenever I hear that sultry voice, all I can picture is it being used to get me into deep trouble. Like when she told my father I'd climbed out my bedroom window and gone to a college party when I was sixteen. She wanted to get even because I wouldn't take her with me."

She stared at him, still not following.

"Lady Love is Kelsey," he explained.

"Your sister?"

"Yes. My rotten, bratty little sister who once painted pink hearts and flowers on my skateboard because I wouldn't let her borrow it."

"Oh! Wow. Your sister does have a cool job," she said, remembering his comment from the day before. She took another bite of breakfast. Thinking of his voice on the tape recorder the night before, and all the other times he'd made her quiver with his evocative whispers, she continued, "Now that I think about it, the two of you have a lot in common. Your voice is as powerful as hers."

"I perform for private audiences only. And only because you make me lose my mind."

"Ditto," she replied, then took another bite of breakfast. She really had worked up an appetite the night before. After sipping juice, she said, "I can see why it might be uncomfortable for you to listen to her show."

"Usually it's fine," Nate replied. "Some nights I laugh about it, imagining what her husband, Mitch, is going through at home with their two kids while she's on the radio titillating half the eastern seaboard. Her show's been syndicated, you know."

She nodded. "Mitch is your friend, right?"

"My best friend. He practically grew up with us. Anyway, I've never listened to the show with a woman before, and I definitely didn't want to be hearing my kid sister while watching you."

She bit her lip as she remembered exactly what he was watching her *do.* The heat in his expression told her he was remembering, too.

"So," she finally said after nervously taking a few more bites of egg, "your sister ended up becoming a hot radio deejay, and you write sexy relationship stuff in a men's magazine. What do your parents think of that?"

He grinned. "They're very supportive. Now that they know Mitch is around to make sure Kelsey doesn't get hurt by some wacko fan or something, they don't worry about her so much anymore."

"And you?"

"Well, they're still waiting for some woman to come along and show me the error of my ways in the romance department. They haven't given up on me settling down."

Lacey held her breath, but he didn't continue. Finally she said, "I wonder what they'll say when they read our crossover articles."

"What do you mean?"

"When they see you've been firmly convinced by our research that most men are *not* happier being single and playing the field."

"They're not?"

She glared and considered tossing a piece of toast at his smirking face. "No, they're not."

"So you still believe every guy who drools over the magazine centerfold secretly has dreams of the mini-van and the white picket fence with the girl next door?"

She found his amusement incredibly annoying. "And you still really believe women trap men into unwanted commitments to justify the fact that they're every bit as horny as men?"

"Women *are* every bit as horny as men." His voice challenged her to deny it.

"Men *do* secretly want commitment and a life mate," she retorted.

They stared at each other over the food for several long seconds. Then Nate slowly raised his coffee mug to his lips and sipped from it. He murmured, "Well, I guess that's what you and I are going to find out, isn't it?"

"The article," she said, knowing immediately what he meant. "You're still approaching it from your original point of view? That commitment isn't necessary and true love is a fluke?"

"Isn't that what J.T. asked us to do?" His eyes stared intently into hers. "Besides, isn't that exactly what you're going to do, too—defend your views on love and relationships?"

Was she? After last night, after feeling wild, reckless abandon in this man's bed, what kind of hypocrite would she be to say women should hold out for true love and not settle for casual sex? Nate hadn't spoken one word of love to her, nor she to him.

She wasn't that much of a hypocrite. Still, Lacey's basic, deep-down beliefs remained unchanged. No, she hadn't held out for true love, but there was absolutely nothing casual about what she'd shared with Nate the night before. At least not on her part. Maybe he wasn't in love with her, maybe he didn't want to be her life-long partner and soul mate, but he cared about her. She didn't doubt that. No way he could have made love to her the way he did if his feelings weren't involved somehow.

Besides, no matter what he felt, he'd still somehow managed to charm, flirt, cajole and seduce his way into her heart. Drat the man.

"True love is possible," she finally replied. "Tender romance can lead to a lifelong commitment and a happily ever after. Even in today's world." She silently challenged him to deny it.

"Sure it's possible, Lacey."

She breathed a sigh of relief.

"Like it's possible for an honest politician to move into the White House. It's just not the norm."

Nate saw her grit her teeth in frustration and hid a smile. Sometimes Lacey could be so easy to read. She was obviously fighting the urge to throw the last few bits of her egg into his face.

He didn't quite know what she had expected of their conversation, but if she was waiting for him to fall on his knees declaring his true love and proposing their own happily ever after, she'd be waiting a little longer. Nate wasn't that kind of fool.

Because she'd never believe it. Not in a million years would she believe he, Nate Logan, had lost his head over her Friday night on the trampoline, and his heart shortly thereafter. Even though that's exactly what had happened.

It was too soon. Last night had been a huge step for her, a leap in the right direction. But once she walked out the door, once the euphoria of what they'd shared receded, she'd be in her old world. The reality of her childhood and her parents' expectations would crash back in on her. In that reality, in that world, she'd doubt every word he said.

So now was not the time for declarations. Nate could afford patience. After all, his lifetime was at stake here. As he'd decided last night, he wasn't letting her go. Ever.

Plus, even though he had found someone he believed he could love for the rest of his life, he still had a story to write about all the other men on the planet. In his opinion and experience, guys did *not* go out to bars to find women to bear their children. The activity that produced children, well, sure, that was a given. But men searching for soul mates? Nah. It just didn't happen.

Yes, plenty of men settled down, got married, had the house in the burbs and a couple of kids. Considering sixty percent of them cheated and half ended up divorced, however, he had to believe most men really still pined for the caveman days of spreading their seed around.

As a professional journalist, he had an obligation to follow through on his promise to J.T. They had a deal. His boss wanted the magazine battle of the sexes to continue, and Nate wanted to write features for *Men's World*. Personal feelings had no place in the equation at all.

"You're wrong," Lacey finally replied.

"I don't think so."

"Well, like you said, we're going to find out. This

past week has been *interesting*...but not exactly productive. It's time to get to work. We've got three weeks before our deadline."

"I've made a lot of calls, done a lot of phone interviews in the past few days," he said.

"So have I. But we need to go further. Maybe that singles ad idea isn't such a bad one."

Nate shook his head. "Forget it. You're not going out with some guy who responds to a lonely hearts ad."

She crossed her arms and tilted her head. "And why not?"

"Ax-murdering psychos come to mind."

She rolled her eyes. "Do I have to remind you it was your idea?"

"That was before."

"Before what?"

"You know damn well before what," he retorted. "Before last night. Before us."

"Last night has nothing to do with the story, Nate. You made that perfectly clear."

He muttered a silent curse, seeing determination in her eyes. "Lacey, I'm not going to sit back and watch you go out with other men for the sake of a story. Not while we're involved. Do you honestly feel any differently?"

She chewed on the corner of her lip for a second, then finally shook her head. "No, I don't like the idea of me sitting around, twiddling my thumbs, knowing you're out at a club with a bunch of guys on the make."

"So we're agreed," he said with a sigh of relief that she'd seen things his way. "We'll go at it from another angle."

Lacey placed her elbows on the table and rested her chin in the palm of one hand. "There is no other angle.

If we're going to write about what men and women really want, we need to be out there, seeing it firsthand."

An idea hit him. "I just thought of another angle. My sister, Kelsey, wants us to appear on her radio show. Did I mention that? She liked the idea of us talking on the air about our battle of the sexes."

"That's a start," she said with a thoughtful nod. "But it's not enough. I think there's only one solution."

He was almost afraid to ask. "What's that?"

She sat up straight, dropping her hands to the table as if she'd come to a great decision. "Simple. We can't be involved while we write the story."

His jaw fell open.

"Last night was...well, let's say we've done what we've wanted to do since we met. It's out of our systems. The pressure's off. Now we go back to being colleagues and do our jobs."

He snorted. "Yeah, right." Then he noticed she wasn't laughing. "You can't be serious."

"I am totally serious."

"You think last night was it, and we can just forget about it, not want each other anymore now that we've made love again?"

She shook her head. "It's not a question of forgetting. It's simply a matter of...of putting it out of our minds. Keeping focused on the story, not on, well, you know."

Nate couldn't help it—he laughed for a solid thirty seconds. Finally, seeing her glare, he said, "No way. There's no way in hell you can put what happened out of your mind."

"Confident, aren't you?"

"Realistic. You're telling me you can work with me every day for three weeks—talking about sex, interviewing people about sex, being *saturated* with sex—

and not want sex? Hell, I want it just from sitting here having this conversation!"

"Maybe I have better control of my drives than you do."

"Bull," he replied succinctly. "You and I were striking sparks off each other the minute we met. Now that we've explored every inch of each other, had our mouths on each other, done things together I'd never even dreamed of doing with anyone else..." He lowered his voice. "Now that I've been *inside* you...you really think you can simply turn it off?"

Her eyes widened. Her pretty red lips parted as she drew in a few deep breaths. A blush stained her cheeks, and her tight tank top beautifully displayed the sudden hardness of her pert nipples. He had his answer. Not that she'd admit it.

"Face it, Lacey—we wouldn't last a day."

"Maybe you wouldn't."

"I know damn well I wouldn't," he said, running a hand through his hair in frustration. "And you wouldn't, either."

"Is that a challenge?"

He held his hands up, palms out. "No, not a challenge. I am *not* daring you to do this." He knew her too well. She had a competitive spirit. He wasn't about to give her ammunition to implement her insane solution. "I'm merely saying it's a ridiculous idea."

She stood, carried her dishes to the sink and rinsed them. Then she turned, leaning against the counter, and stared at him. Nate didn't like the determined look in her eyes. "Lacey?"

"It might be ridiculous to you, Nate. But it's not to me. There's too much riding on this story for me to risk messing it up. Staying involved with you would *definitely* mess it up. So, this ends now. Today."

"Ends?"

She clarified. "For the duration of the story, at least."

"We're talking weeks."

"Yes. Three weeks. And during that time, I'd sincerely appreciate it if you'd avoid, uh…"

He stood and walked toward her. "Seducing you?"

She nodded. "Exactly."

Nate stepped closer until they were practically nose to nose. Her blue eyes widened, and she took a tiny step back. "I won't set out to seduce you," he said softly.

She looked relieved.

"I won't need to. You won't last twenty-four hours."

SHE LASTED thirty-six. By eleven o'clock Sunday night, Lacey was ready to crawl out of her own skin. If Nate had been in the room, she would have jumped on him. Pounced. Attacked him like a woman on a month-long protein diet going after a king-size Snickers bar.

Fortunately, he was not in the room. She lay alone in her bed, thinking about him. "I can do this," she whispered in the darkness. "I lasted twenty-six years without having good sex, I can go three weeks."

If she'd never spent Friday night with him, she probably could have. Now she had to wonder.

Today certainly hadn't been easy. She'd agreed to accompany Nate to Annapolis—partly for research, partly to prove to him, and to herself, that she could be around him without succumbing to her urge to rip off his shirt and nibble his biceps. She'd managed to avoid grabbing his thick blond hair and kissing him senseless, in spite of the adorably sexy grin on his lips every time he'd looked at her in her tight white shorts and red halter top.

Okay, so she'd been wicked when choosing her outfit. Maybe she had been paying him back a little bit, spicing up the forbidden fruit, to get even with him for not admitting he had feelings for her the previous morning. She *knew* he had feelings for her. Dammit, he'd better have feelings for her, considering she'd fallen so hard for him!

She'd been devastated when he'd said he was sticking with his original theory for the story. She'd gone to bed Friday night with the storybook prince and woken up with the playboy.

"I shoulda shoved you into the bay," she muttered as she thought about their trip to Annapolis.

They'd spent Sunday afternoon scoping out the hangouts near the Naval Academy. Lacey had to admit it—Nate had won this particular round. Every restaurant, bar and shopping center was full of handsome cadets and attractive young women trying to get their attention. Lacey had talked to a few of the women, doing on-the-spot interviews. Most had, unfortunately, backed up Nate's belief. They were on the prowl, looking for a gorgeous guy to hook up with for the summer. There was no mention of love, no expectation of happily ever after.

"They were just girls," she told herself, remembering what it was like to be in college, not even thinking about what would come after graduation.

They'd sure looked like women when they were flirting with Nate, though. She'd had a serious urge to pinch one Britney Spears wannabe who'd tried to give Nate her phone number.

It's your own fault.

She was the one who'd insisted they make it clear they were colleagues, not a couple. Nate hadn't appeared to mind. She'd seen the amusement in his eyes while she frowned at all the women who flirted with him. He'd started to mind, though, when he'd realized Lacey was receiving her fair share of attention. She'd seriously thought Nate was going to have it out with one cute sailor who'd tried to talk her into coming to a party near the base. Nate had muttered about muscle heads dressed in white for the rest of the evening.

When he took her home, insisting on walking her to the door of her apartment, she'd held her breath. Would he try to kiss her? What if he asked to come in? Lying here, a few hours later, she conceded that if he had, she'd probably have said yes.

He hadn't asked.

She didn't just *want* him. It was more than want, this feeling preventing her from falling asleep. This was *need*. A painful, intense need pounding throughout her entire body. Lacey almost resented him for showing her the passion of which she was capable. Almost.

As the hot night wore on, the dark minutes stretching into hours, Lacey remembered more of what he'd taught her, more of what she'd learned about herself Friday night. Until, finally, she relieved the pressure alone.

She supposed that was one thing she had to thank him for. Nate Logan had made her realize she was allowed to touch herself.

But her hands were a damn poor substitute for *him*.

10

BY THE END of two weeks, Nate was ready to cry uncle. He would have done about anything—including sitting through a ten-hanky chick flick—if it got Lacey to give up on her plan. The only thing that had stopped him from grabbing her and kissing her until she tore off her own clothes was his promise. He'd agreed not to seduce her.

"You idiot," he muttered Friday night as he drove downtown.

"What'd I do?" Raul asked from the passenger seat.

"Nothing. I was talking to myself."

They were headed for a popular, trendy restaurant and bar, an after-hours hangout that had a reputation as a meat market. Lacey and Venus were probably already there. Lacey had e-mailed him an hour ago, saying they were going ahead with his original idea to check out the local singles scene. She told him he could show up, too, but only if he sat at another table.

"Is she crazy?" He didn't expect Raul to answer. "Doesn't she know what kind of guys hang out in places like that?"

Raul snorted a laugh, ignoring Nate's glare. "I'm sure she'll be fine. She can take care of herself. Besides, she's not alone. Amazon woman is there with her."

Nate shot him a look of disgust. "And that's supposed to make me feel better?"

Lacey was vulnerable right now, one walking case of sexual anticipation. Just like Nate. He hit the gas.

"Slow down," Raul said as he quickly buckled his seat belt. "You're gonna get us killed."

Still thinking about the past several days, Nate ignored him. He couldn't believe Lacey hadn't caved in yet. They'd spent hours together, every day, some evenings as well, debating, interviewing, making phone calls, researching case studies and statistics. They'd lived on Chinese take-out and adrenaline, both too keyed up to sleep, both too stubborn to relent.

They'd scoped out trendy restaurants, college campuses, grocery stores and libraries. He'd talked to dozens of people, old and young, married and single. Lacey had done the same.

J.T. had mentioned their assignment during an interview on a local TV news program last week. The story had garnered a great deal of attention, even nationwide. Celebrities suddenly returned phone calls. Experts crawled out of the woodwork to throw in their two cents worth on the whole man-woman-sex-love debate.

Not that Nate much cared. The assignment had become a chore, a hurdle to overcome so he and Lacey could get back to where they'd been fourteen days before.

The sexual intensity, so powerful from the night they met, had become almost overwhelming now that they both knew what it could be like between them. With every shared smile, every casual brush of a hand or covetous glance, Nate felt his control slip further away. Lacey's, too. Those powder-blue eyes couldn't hide her feelings. She was as on edge, needy and hot as he.

Still, she wouldn't back down. They hadn't so much

as kissed since that Saturday morning in his apartment. Flirted, yes. Made some seriously steamy eye contact and exchanged lots of verbal innuendo, oh, yeah. Nothing else, though.

The only good thing he could say about the past two weeks of his life was that he hadn't blown up into a million bits of sexually frustrated flesh. Of course a man couldn't explode from sexual tension—though Nate thought he'd come pretty damn close.

He supposed a woman couldn't, either. But it wasn't pleasant to think of Lacey, *his* recently awakened, sensual Lacey, sitting in a bar with a bunch of randy businessmen—especially with Venus the love goddess sitting beside her.

"There it is." Raul pointed. He sounded relieved.

There had been one other benefit to their enforced celibacy. Nate knew he'd fallen crazy in love with Lacey Clark. While he'd never before been able to verbalize the exact definition of love, there was no doubt in his mind that's what he felt now. He'd suspected it the night they met, been more sure of it when they'd made love. After two weeks in her company, watching her come out of her shell, seeing the saucy, sassy, confident Lacey emerge from her self-imposed boundaries, he knew he'd found the woman of his dreams.

He merely had to wait her out. And write this bloody article.

When they entered the bar, it didn't take long to spot the two women. "They're surrounded," Nate said with a grimace.

"No caveman stuff. Do what she asked. We'll sit right over here," Raul said as he steered Nate away from the table where Lacey and Venus talked with three suit-wearing jerks.

"If that guy with the glasses leans over to look down her shirt again, he's gonna be swallowing some of his teeth," Nate muttered as he allowed Raul to push him into a chair.

"I never knew Mr. So Many Bimbos So Little Time Logan was capable of a mortal emotion like jealousy," Raul said, grinning.

"I'm not jealous. I trust Lacey."

Raul looked skeptical.

"I *do*. I just don't trust any of the guys around her."

Raul's smile remained firmly in place as they each ordered a beer. Nate waited until Lacey's eyes finally found his across the crowded room. She gave him a tiny, flirtatious wink, then turned her attention to the men standing beside her table.

"She's working on the story," Raul said, probably noticing Nate staring as Lacey earnestly questioned a dark-haired man in a tailored suit. "Remember that little thing called your job?"

"How could I forget." Nate sipped his beer. "Who'da thought an assignment about sex would be so sexually frustrating?"

"I think Lacey had the right idea. You've obviously got a lot of potential information right in this room—a prime opportunity to find out what women are really looking for." He grinned confidently. "Other than a night with me, of course."

Nate shook his head. "You're a piece of work."

Raul didn't reply. His eyes widened, and he looked past Nate to the front door. Nate didn't even have to look to know some hot-looking lady had just entered. Raul had that come-to-Papa look on his face.

Sighing, he noted Raul was right. He had a job to do. He turned, glanced over his shoulder and saw four giggly females walking in. They sat down at the next table, casting quick glances around the bar before throwing wide, welcoming smiles toward Nate and Raul. Four average, probably single, twenty-something women living and loving in the city of Baltimore. *Okay, Logan, time to get to work.*

LACEY nearly came out of her seat when a big-chested brunette and her three twitty cohorts pulled their chairs up to Nate's table and made themselves comfortable.

"Cool it, sweetie," Venus advised, placing a restraining hand on Lacey's arm. "You started this, remember?"

Yes, she had. Though, suddenly, seeing Nate laugh at something Miss Silicone Implants said, she couldn't remember why.

"Like I said, you are absolutely right," a dark-haired man in a charcoal-gray suit said. He'd been the first to approach them when they'd arrived at the bar an hour before. Lacey had managed to steer the conversation toward relationships.

"I dream about coming home at night to that one special woman," he continued. "Talking about our day, tucking our kids in at night, then giving in to the passion that has sustained our marriage all our lives."

"Watch out, I think I'm gonna barf," Venus muttered in Lacey's ear. She, apparently, had had quite enough of this lecherous creep who'd used every opportunity he could to touch Lacey.

"Oh, me, too," the pipsqueak said. Lacey had dubbed the one in the thick glasses the pipsqueak. He hadn't tried to touch. He seemed happy standing above them, sneaking peeks down her blouse, getting all tongue-tied and drooly whenever Venus looked at him. "I dream of finding a woman just like my mother."

"I think I hear her calling you," Venus mumbled as she took a healthy sip of her strawberry daiquiri.

Lacey bit the inside of her cheek. This was proving to be a waste of time. These men weren't taking her questions seriously—they were trying to pick her up. Not that she'd expected much else, given the reputation of the place. She should really feel guilty for intentionally goading Nate by arranging this evening's research trip.

"Excuse me," a waitress said as she placed a glass of champagne on the table. "The gentleman over there sent this."

Nate. Looking across the room, Lacey met his eyes. He stared at her, ignoring the mountain of synthetic cleavage resting on his table. A half smile played about his gorgeous lips, his gaze conveying tenderness and humor. And need. Lacey's heart skipped a beat.

"He sent this, as well."

She took the napkin the waitress offered. Turning slightly for privacy, she read it. "Careful not to let the little one get too close to the window. It's still light out. If the sun shines through those glasses, he might burn the place down."

She grinned. "Got a pen?"

Venus dug through her bag and came up with one. "From trampoline man, I assume? He's looking quite *delish* tonight."

Lacey nodded as Venus leaned closer to whisper, "Then again, considering the dregs who've been hitting on us, even your little lackey is looking good by comparison."

Lacey glanced at her friend. Venus was making

some serious eye contact...with Raul. When Venus pulled a tube of lipstick out and pursed her lips to apply it, Lacey seriously thought Raul was going to fall out of his chair, he leaned over so far. Then, with a pout, Venus mouthed, "Where's *my* champagne?"

Lacey snorted with laughter when Raul immediately threw his arm up in the air, beckoning for the waitress. "You're bad."

"Bad's the only way to be," Venus said in a Mae West purr.

Lacey finished writing her note and asked the waitress to give it to Nate. She watched as it was delivered, saw him grin when he read what she'd written. "I think I hear your table groaning from over here under the weight of those things."

He stood, saying something to the women, who suddenly looked very disappointed. Raul stood, as well. They were, quite obviously, on their way over.

Venus noticed, too. Turning to the three men remaining next to their table, she said, "All right, boys, I think that's all for tonight. Be good enough to shove off now, would you?"

The man in the gray suit widened his eyes in surprise. "But I thought we were just getting friendly...."

"Oh, give it up," Lacey interrupted. She felt as uninterested in continuing her story research as Venus. "I see the white mark on your ring finger. Put your wedding band back on and get home to your wife. There might still be time to put your kids to bed together and thrill in your marital passion."

"Well done," Venus murmured with a chuckle.

The man crossed his arms to hide his left hand. Then he and the second man—probably also married—

walked away. That left just the guy with the sneaky eyes and the drool-coated lips.

"I'm really single," he offered. He snuck another quick peek down Lacey's blouse.

"Sorry, dear," Venus said with an evil smile. "We're due back at the dominatrix academy in an hour."

The man's eyes widened behind the Coke-bottle glasses.

"Can we join you?" Raul asked.

"At the academy?" Venus said without missing a beat. "I don't think you could handle it, little boy."

"You might be surprised by what I can handle," Raul replied as he plopped into the vacant seat next to Venus.

"Better luck next time, pal," Nate said as he brushed past, then sat down next to Lacey. Mr. Roving Eyes quickly walked away.

"My, my, the people you run into in this place," Lacey said with a grin as she sipped her champagne.

"You set this up intentionally."

She shrugged. "You'll never prove it."

"It worked. I was ready to pound that first guy into mashed potatoes if he touched you again."

"Well, I guess I should admit I envisioned voodoo dolls and stick pins when I saw Miss Double D fawning all over you."

He chuckled. "So we're jealous. I have to confess that's never happened to me with anyone but you. What does that prove?"

She paused, holding his stare. "Maybe you want me all to yourself until we finish what we started?"

He waited before answering. "I don't think it's just that. This isn't about male ego. I think there's more to it."

Lacey almost held her breath. "Like what?"

He took a long time drinking his beer, then looking around the room. Finally, he leaned close to Lacey and tenderly smoothed her hair back. When he ran his fingers across her cheek, Lacey shivered at the contact, fighting not to close her eyes and moan. "Nathan?" she prompted.

"I don't think I'll tell you yet," he whispered, his breath warm and arousing against her skin. He nibbled her earlobe, nearly bringing her off the seat. "I'll tell you next Friday. After we meet our deadline."

FRIDAY couldn't come soon enough for Lacey. She worked like one possessed all week, and by the time she'd finished typing her article at ten o'clock Thursday night, she felt completely exhausted. She considered it the best thing she'd ever written. She figured it was definitely going to raise some eyebrows, though. Including J.T.'s.

When the phone rang at eleven, she knew full well who was calling. "Are you finished?" she said as soon as she answered.

"Not quite," Nate admitted with a chuckle. "You?"

Lacey curled in her bed. "Uh-huh. I'm beat."

"Wish I was there to give you a back rub."

She nearly purred at the thought. "Rain check?"

"Absolutely. Tomorrow night. After the show."

Lacey had nearly forgotten about their plans for Friday night. She and Nate were scheduled to appear on his sister's radio show, "Night Whispers." Not for research, since their articles would be turned in already, but for promotion. J.T. was scheduled to phone in for an on-the-air interview.

"I'll see you tomorrow then. At the radio station."

"And then?"

She smiled. "Your place."

"I'm counting on it," he replied with vehemence.

Lacey hand-delivered her article directly to J.T.'s office the next day. Though he was out, she sat behind his desk, grabbed some paper and wrote him a note. "Here you go. Thanks for the eye-opening assignment. I learned a lot. Don't forget our deal."

She took the rest of the afternoon off. As she drove to her favorite hair and nail salon for some serious primping, Lacey flipped on the stereo. She popped in a Rod Stewart CD. "Tonight's the night," she sang along, pleased at the appropriateness of the music. Yes, tonight was definitely the night. After three weeks of foreplay, she was more than ready to get back to basics with Nate Logan. In his bed. In his arms. "In his life," she mused.

The past three weeks really had been eye-opening for Lacey. She'd loved the challenge of their assignment and the verbal sparring in which they'd engaged. She'd loved his stupid jokes, his neck rubs, his constant good humor, not to mention their late-night phone calls and the mornings he'd show up with fresh bagels. She'd loved the way she felt when she looked across her office and saw him standing in the doorway, leaning against the jamb, smiling at her. She loved...Nate Logan. Truly, madly, with her whole heart.

The sexual tension had been overwhelming. But somehow Lacey had survived it, moving beyond it to enjoy the laughter and friendship between them. What definitely had not survived were her doubts about her feelings. This wasn't passion-induced euphoria or attraction. Yes, she felt those things, but, even more, she'd come to know and love Nate the man.

Tonight, after the radio show, she was going to let him know it. Whether he returned her feelings or not, she felt ready to admit her own. A month ago she wouldn't have. The Lacey from before the night of J.T.'s party would have protected her heart, not risked rejection, not allowed him to have any power over her whatsoever. She would have played it safe, been patient, waited for him to make the first move like good girls are supposed to do. Not now. The new Lacey was going to tell him she loved him.

Then she planned to thoroughly seduce the man.

NATE ARRIVED at the station early, wanting a chance to visit with Kelsey. He hadn't seen her in several days, since he'd been so busy with the assignment. He found her running around frantically, preparing for the evening's show.

"Haven't you ever learned the value of organization?" he asked her when she paused to give him a quick kiss on the cheek.

"Nice to see you, too." She punched his upper arm. "That's for not coming to see your niece and nephew in two weeks."

He rubbed his arm. "Sorry. I've been a little distracted."

"No kidding," she said with a disgruntled expression. "Who is she? And please tell me she's at least of legal drinking age. I'd like to be able to leave the liquor cabinet unlocked when you bring a date over to meet me."

Nate snorted. "Ha, ha, smart-ass. Thanks for the vote of confidence. She's not only over twenty-one, she's actually a beautiful, brilliant, successful writer."

"Luckily, I know your tastes in reading have

changed," Kelsey replied, "so I assume she doesn't write jokes for bubblegum wrappers."

He rolled his eyes.

"Okay, okay," she admitted, "I heard it in your voice when you told me about this assignment you're doing with Lacey Clark. It's her, right?"

He nodded.

"You nuts about her?"

"That pretty much sums it up."

A pleased expression crossed Kelsey's face. "I'm glad for you, Nate. I'm so glad you found someone who totally blew you away. I knew it would happen someday."

"Just like I knew you'd never have eyes for anyone but Mitch." Nate threw an affectionate arm across her shoulders.

"Have you told her yet?" Kelsey asked. "You know, not every woman has the confidence to be, uh, blunt about her feelings. I made all the overtures to Mitch, but I hear there are actually some women out there who like the man to be the pursuer."

Nate laughed as he followed his whirlwind little sister to her office in the radio station building. "Moving up in the world, I see," he said as he noted the size of the room and the view of the harbor out her window.

"I mean it, Nate. If you're crazy about her, don't you think you ought to tell her? Then again, maybe you shouldn't. Maybe you should wait until after I meet her, because if I don't like her, she's history."

"You'll like her," Nate predicted. "And I plan to tell her tonight after the show, when I give her a copy of my article."

"You have a copy with you?"

He nodded warily, recognizing the sparkle in his sister's eyes. As expected, Kelsey didn't relent until she'd gotten him to let her look at the article. Giving up, Nate pulled the manila envelope out of his briefcase and handed it to her. He sat down in a chair and watched as Kelsey leaned against her desk reading the piece.

She smiled as she read. Then she started laughing. When she was finished, she handed it back to him, then grabbed a tissue and wiped her eyes. "I can't wait to meet her."

LACEY PREPARED more for the evening she had planned after "Night Whispers" than she did for the interview itself. Though it seemed silly, since Nate had a great supply of lingerie hanging in his coat closet, she couldn't help visiting her favorite shop to pick up something new.

Not that she'd be wearing it for very long. If Nate was half as frantic as she, it wouldn't matter if she showed up in an old lady's flowered housecoat and curlers. Still...the emerald green silk thong was irresistible. Plus it somehow seemed appropriate.

When Lacey arrived at the office building that housed the station, she was directed to a studio control room. She heard Nate's laughter before she entered, plus a woman's low, sultry voice she recognized from listening to "Night Whispers." For the first time, Lacey felt a little nervous. She was about to meet a member of Nate's family. Not only that, she was coming face to face with the woman who'd inspired her to be utterly outrageous in Nate's living room a few weeks before.

"Lacey," Nate said as he spotted her through the open doorway. Taking a deep breath, Lacey allowed him to lead her into the room.

A half hour later, when they were about to go into

the studio to go live on the air, Lacey couldn't believe she'd ever worried. Nate's sister was charming—friendly, warm, with wit to spare. She'd delighted in telling Lacey about some of Nate's childhood troubles, and Lacey had loved every word.

"Okay, it's time to go in," Kelsey said as her producer came into the control booth and introduced himself. "You're clear on what'll happen, right? The topic tonight is the battle of the sexes, and my interview with you two will take up the entire first half hour. Then we hook up with J.T. for a few minutes."

Lacey nodded and followed Kelsey into the studio, taking one of the empty seats. Putting on a set of headphones, she scooted her rolling chair close to one of the extra microphones and watched as Nate did the same.

When Kelsey leaned into the mike and began to speak, Lacey was amazed at the change. The warm kid sister she'd met thirty minutes before had been replaced by the smooth-talking temptress who'd seduced the city.

"Good evening, Baltimore, this is Lady Love. Tonight we're discussing the battle of the sexes. I have as my special guests two well-known columnists from right here in the Charm City. Lacey Clark and Nate Logan have been spicing up the pages of two of our favorite magazines for months. And now they're here to spice up 'Night Whispers.'" She laughed across the microphone and glanced toward Lacey and Nate. "A month ago, I might have had to wear flak gear in here. But let's just say things appear a little *friendlier* now between our favorite dueling duo."

Lacey and Nate exchanged amused glances.

The interview sped by quickly. As expected, Nate was his flirtatious, charming self. Now that she knew him so well, Lacey recognized that he was performing. He played a role, much as when he wrote some obnoxious comment in his column. His readers expected it. The radio audience expected the same.

While she would have loved for him to proclaim his complete change in attitude—then go on and profess his undying love for her—she knew he wouldn't. Whether Nate loved her or not, he was still, first and foremost, a journalist. J.T. and *Men's World* expected the sexy, freewheeling playboy, and that's what he gave them. Period. In print and on the radio. To come across like a mushy, sappy romantic would go against everything he'd ever written for *Men's World*. She understood why he wouldn't. And, to be honest, she had a great time giving back as good as she got during their on-air debate.

"When we come back on the air, we're going to be joined by publisher J.T. Birmingham, who's going to give us his perspective on Nate and Lacey's assignment," Kelsey said about a half hour into the show. "With his romantic track record, I bet he'll have something interesting to add to our conversation."

Lacey couldn't help it. She immediately tensed up at the thought of J.T. getting on the radio and talking about his relationships, especially *certain* relationships.

During the commercial break, Kelsey complimented them on the interview, saying they were almost finished. Lacey looked at the clock, noting it was after ten-thirty. Yes, almost done. A few more minutes and they'd be out of here. The rest of the night could commence. She could hardly wait.

Nate caught her eye and gave her a definitely sultry look. No doubt he was thinking exactly the same thing she'd been.

Just before the break ended, Lacey heard a tapping on the glass window of the booth. She glanced over to see Kelsey's producer making a rolling motion with his arm. "Brian doesn't have J.T. on the line yet," Kelsey said, interpreting the gestures. "Gotta stretch a little bit."

"Welcome back, Baltimore," Kelsey said into the microphone. "This is Lady Love, and we're having a fascinating discussion with our guests, Lacey Clark and Nathan Logan. Their print debate has come alive right here in the WAJO studios. We're also about to be joined by magazine publisher J.T. Birmingham." She cast an evil grin toward Nate and Lacey. "Before we go live with J.T., I want to tell you something." She paused deliberately. "Someone in this studio is a fraud."

Lacey cast a quick, anxious glance toward Nate. He was frowning at his sister.

"One of my guests has a secret. You all know I just love secrets, right? Especially secrets involving passionate love affairs. Before the show tonight," Kelsey continued, obviously completely unconcerned by her brother's frown, "Nate told me something. It seems that one of the people in this room is *not* who they purport to be...not the person the world thinks they are. Someone's *hiding* something."

From his seat in the studio, Nate mentally uttered a curse. *Kelsey, you rotten little monster!* He knew instantly what she was getting at. His kid sister was about to tell the world, on live radio, that he, Nate Logan, was in love with his nemesis Lacey Clark—before he had a chance to make that declaration on his own.

Typical of Kelsey. If they weren't in the middle of a live radio broadcast, he'd throw a hand over her mouth and bribe her with chocolate to get her to shut the hell up, just like he had when they were kids. Kelsey had always taken fiendish delight in playing the obnoxious-baby-sister role to the hilt. It enabled her to get away with murder! And Nate had learned at a young age that arguing never worked. Reasoning never worked. Only bribery could get Kelsey Logan to quiet down once she was on a roll.

Nate wished he'd never let her sucker him into showing her his article, which made it very clear—to her and to everyone else—that he, Nate Logan, had fallen ass over elbows in love with Lacey. Ah, well, he supposed there were worse ways to propose to the woman he was crazy about than on live radio with thousands of titillated Baltimore residents listening in.

ON HER SIDE of the studio, Lacey glanced between brother and sister, a sick feeling in her stomach. Nate shook his head, rubbing a weary hand over his brow, as if resigned to whatever Kelsey was about to say.

Lacey didn't know exactly what was happening; she just knew the room suddenly felt hot and close. Though they were expected to interact with J.T. during his phone interview, Lacey wanted nothing more than to leave. She leaned toward Nate to tell him exactly that. Before she could do so, Kelsey got a signal from her producer.

"It appears we now have J.T. Birmingham on the line," the deejay said into the microphone.

Lacey kept her hands clenched in her lap during Lady Love's interview with J.T. She hadn't liked Kelsey's comments about secrets. Obviously the first thought that came to mind was Lacey's situation, though she knew it had to be something else. Nate wouldn't have told his sister about Lacey's past. She couldn't imagine, however, what Kelsey had been talking about.

After the first few minutes of the interview with J.T., Lacey began to relax. Whatever Nate had discussed with his sister before the show, the subject seemed to be forgotten now.

"So, Mr. Birmingham, you must be pretty proud of your stars here," Kelsey said. "I've seen national TV coverage of their 'he said, she said' debates this week."

"I'm very proud," J.T. replied. Lacey could envision his chest expanding. "I can't wait to read both articles. I was out of the office today and haven't seen them yet."

"So you've had a real hands-on involvement with this project, I take it?"

"Absolutely. I have to admit, it was my idea. Nate's been such a wonderful addition to *Men's World,* we wanted to give him a chance to shine even more."

"And Lacey?" Kelsey prompted.

"Of course, she's phenomenal," J.T. replied. Lacey heard the tenderness in his voice as his bluster faded. He sounded very sincere. "What can I say about Lacey? She's brilliant, gifted, a dream come true."

Lacey felt Nate's stare and glanced over to see him watching her closely. Feeling moisture in her eyes, she blinked rapidly. Kelsey obviously noticed, as well, because a sudden sweet and understanding smile crossed her face.

"I'm sure she is," Kelsey said. "Of course, you have to say that, don't you? As her proud father?"

There was no immediate response—not from J.T. who merely gasped on live radio. Not from Nate, whose eyes were wide with shock and whose mouth hung open in horror.

Certainly not from Lacey. She couldn't possibly speak with her heart in her throat, not to mention the world exploding all around her.

Nate watched her face crumble. "Lacey, wait," he said as she yanked her headphones off and jumped out of her chair. He had no idea what on earth had just happened in the studio, how his sister could possibly have known about J.T. and Lacey, but he had a pretty good idea what Lacey was thinking right now.

"Get out of my way," she snarled before rushing out.

He cast a glare that promised retribution at Kelsey, who, he had to admit, looked completely stunned by her guests' reaction. There was no time for explanations, however. Nate took off after the woman he loved—the woman who had just looked at him with pain and betrayal in her beautiful blue eyes.

She was running through the darkened office building, where only a few night workers and a security guard were visible. He finally caught up with her in the lobby. "Please, listen to me," he said, grabbing her arm.

She yanked away from his touch. "I don't want to hear it. You set me up. I can't believe you set me up. Why, Nate? Why'd you do it? To boost your sister's ratings? To get more readers for the articles?" She shoved at his chest with both hands. "Dammit, I trusted you!"

When she reached for the front door, Nate blocked her with his body. "I did not betray you, Lacey."

"What do you call it? A slip of the tongue? An accident?"

"No, you don't understand. I *didn't* tell Kelsey."

She snorted in disbelief. "Sure you didn't. That was the big secret she was talking about earlier." She turned and ran her hands through her hair. "What am I going to do? I have to go. I have to call my mother. That's if I can get into my apartment without being attacked by reporters. I'll bet they're tracking down my address right now."

"Lacey, this is not a catastrophe," he said, trying to calm her down. "Yes, it's awful that you have to deal with it now, rather than at the end of the year, but you've known this had to happen sooner or later."

"Get out of my way." She wouldn't look at him. "I've got to figure out what to do."

He didn't budge. "It is not your fault, Lacey. This situation started before you were born, and you're not the person who has to take care of it anymore."

"So you suggest I forget it? Just let my family fall apart? Ruin everything for my mother and grandparents?"

He mentally cursed. She'd been carrying this burden for years. If her parents were here right now, he would cheerfully tell them all to go straight to hell for what they'd done to her. "You're loving and loyal and caring, Lacey. I wouldn't change that about you for the world. But you've *changed*. You're stronger now, able to make your own choices."

Tears flowed freely down her cheeks. "Do you think I'd choose to have my scandalous family history revealed on live radio with no warning whatsoever?"

"No, but it's done," he said softly, reaching to her cheek to brush away a tear. She pulled back from his hand. He continued, "Everyone has to live with it. Your parents have to come to grips with choices they made before you were born. You can't go back to that place. You can't let them close you in again. You've come out of that box and you need to deal with this like the woman you *are*, not the girl you *were*."

She looked like he'd slapped her. "So you think because you and I slept together you know me inside out, huh? You know the real me better than anyone else in my life?"

He held her stare. Finally, he nodded. "Yeah. I do. And I don't want to lose the real you. You've got to make a choice, Lacey. Move gloriously forward. Be supportive and understanding to your family while still being true to yourself. Acknowledge that you're not responsible for the choices and happiness of everyone around you." He paused. "Or move backward. Be ashamed. Hide the truth. Let them make you their dark secret again."

She bit her lip, trying to blink away her tears.

Nate cupped her face, slid his fingers into the silky softness of her hair and pleaded with her. "Please, move forward, Lacey. With me. Be the woman I've fallen in love with."

She gasped, raising a hand to her chest. "That's not fair, Logan. How dare you say that to me now, when you've pulled the rug out from under me? When you've betrayed me?"

"I haven't." He tilted her chin with his index finger and forced her to look into his eyes. "I'm giving you my word. I did *not* tell Kelsey that J.T. is your father."

She stared at him. Nate met her gaze openly, silently urging her to believe in him. They'd come to know each other so well in the past month, she *had* to trust him, had to be the open, honest, loving woman he'd come to know, who followed her heart and her instincts instead of her doubts and misgivings.

After a pause that seemed to last forever, her eyes shifted. "I don't believe you." She pulled away. "Now I have to go figure out what to do about this nightmare." Turning, she walked out the door.

Nate died a little inside as he acknowledged the truth. He'd taken a gamble by admitting his love for her. He'd gambled, and he'd lost.

His Lacey was gone.

11

HER MOTHER, Donna, had already called twice by the time Lacey got home. One of Donna's old college friends lived in Baltimore and had been listening to the show. "The phone lines are crackling tonight," Lacey muttered. Here and probably in Smeltsville, Indiana, too.

In the first message, her mother asked Lacey to call right away to tell her what had happened. In the second, she said *not* to call tonight. That meant she'd told Lacey's stepfather.

Lacey's first impulse was to get in her car and drive to Indiana. She resisted it. In spite of the pain of the confrontation with Nate at the radio station, she had been listening to what he'd said. He'd been right, in some respects. She couldn't do anything to help her mother at this particular minute. Hell, she couldn't even help herself.

Her heart hurt. Lacey didn't think she'd ever, in her life, felt such a deep sense of loss—not even on the night she'd learned her father wasn't really her father.

Losing Nate, believing he'd betrayed her, knowing she could not be the person he wanted her to be...she'd never imagined she could feel such pain.

LACEY DIDN'T get a chance to talk to her mother until late Saturday. She avoided calls from the press all day long, not picking up the phone if she didn't recognize the number on her caller ID box. Nate's number never came up.

She spoke with her father once. They had a difficult conversation—J.T. was clearly hurt by Lacey's dismay over what had happened. "You know, there might be some people in the world who wouldn't mind having it revealed that I'm their father, rather than that sanctimonious reverend your mother married."

Lacey sighed. "J.T., I know you're having a hard time understanding this. I'm sorry if it seems like I'm ashamed of you. I'm not."

"It does seem that way and has for a long time."

A month ago, Lacey would have bitten her lip, shed a few tears and pleaded for his forgiveness and understanding. Somehow, today, her response was different. "Welcome to my world," she said softly.

"What?" He sounded shocked.

She cleared her throat. "You heard me. Maybe I understand how you're feeling, J.T., because I've felt that way myself."

"You can't think I was anything but thrilled to find you!"

She sighed. "How could I *not* think that, J.T.?"

"I loved and wanted you from the minute you wrote me." He sounded indignant. "It was your mother and her husband who—"

"Hold on a sec," she interrupted him. "I was there, remember? You were perfectly happy letting me into your world for two weeks every summer. You loved playing dad, spoiling me rotten, then getting back to your regularly scheduled life for the rest of the year." She'd shocked him into silence. "I know you love me, J.T.," she continued gently. "I love you, too. But let's be honest about this—a full-time teenage daughter would have put a real cramp in your lifestyle. You were quite happy with Mom's solution. *All* of you seemed quite happy with it."

Finally, after a long, drawn-out pause, he said softly, "Everyone except you?"

Lacey never answered his question. She was still thinking about it later that day when her mother finally called. "Mom, are you all right? I've been waiting to hear from you all day."

"Everything's fine, Lacey," Donna replied. "Your father and I have had a nice talk."

Lacey knew she meant her stepfather. Her mother never called her real father anything but J.T. "Dad took it okay?"

Donna let out a shrill laugh. "Oh, yes. He went over to talk to your grandparents. He's not back yet."

Lacey cringed. "What about Jake?"

"We told your brother this morning. I think he'll be fine in a few days."

"I'll call him."

"That would be nice, Lacey, I'm sure he'd love to hear from you. But wait until Monday. He's staying with a friend now."

Lacey understood what that meant. "He'll come around, just give him time. What about Dad's congregation?"

Her mother laughed again, and again Lacey didn't like the sound. "As a matter of fact, the timing is not so bad. Your father plans to rework his sermon for tomorrow's services. He's going to admit everything and use our marriage as an example of the power of forgiveness."

Lacey closed her eyes and sighed. "I'm sorry."

"Why? It's fine! I'm just thankful I married someone so understanding and forgiving."

Lacey couldn't bite back her retort. "You must be joking." She heard silence on the phone. "Mom, he's been punishing you since the day I was born."

"Lacey Clark!"

"Be honest—with yourself, at least, if not with me. Standing in that pulpit and proclaiming his goodness for forgiving his sinning wife? What is that if not more punishment? God, I'd rather spend my life alone than stay with a man who said he forgave but never even *tried* to forget—and never let you forget it, either!"

Her mother's shocked silence finally became tears. Lacey started crying right along with her, apologizing for her harshness, almost wishing she'd left it alone and not spoken her mind. After all, she'd gone many years without saying what she thought.

Finally, after a few minutes, her mother managed to shock her in return. "You're right, Lacey. I know you are. I did something selfish and foolish when I was young—just a dumb teenage military bride who spent a total of three weeks with her husband the first year of her marriage."

Lacey remained silent. Her mother had never volunteered details about her affair with J.T.

"I went to visit a friend in the big city, and a handsome, wealthy man swept me off my feet."

"Mom, you were a kid," Lacey said, hearing her mother's self-recrimination. "Don't tear yourself up over this anymore."

Her mother sniffed, obviously drying her tears. "I know. You're right. I deeply regret hurting Charles, and I'm thankful he didn't end our marriage when he found out I was pregnant. But I've been apologizing and trying to make it up to him for more than two decades. I think I've been punished long enough."

"Yes, Mom, you have."

By the time they'd finished their telephone conversation, Lacey felt closer to her mother than she had in years. She realized something else, too, about the way she'd challenged her mother to admit the truth—Nate would have been proud of her.

WHEN LACEY ARRIVED in her office early Monday morning, she was shocked to find Nate's sister, Kelsey, waiting for her. She wasn't alone. Sitting on Kelsey's lap was a little girl, probably about two years old, of obvious Oriental descent. Another child, a baby dressed in blue, lay in a stroller.

"Good morning, Lacey," said Nate's sister. "I hope you don't mind me showing up like this. I came to apologize. I truly didn't realize I was hurting you when I made that comment about J.T." Kelsey spoke in a rush, as if afraid Lacey was going to throw her out of the room before she could finish.

Lacey closed her office door, dropped her purse onto her desk, then looked at the little ones. "Your children?"

Kelsey nodded, smiling with pride as she introduced her daughter, Mulan, and her son, Ryan. "I found out I was pregnant with Ryan the month after we got back from China with Mulan," Kelsey admitted with a grin. "Two in diapers is a challenge."

Lacey couldn't help but smile at the little girl wrapped in her mother's arms. "They're beautiful."

"Thank you. Lacey, I really am sorry. I'm not sure what planet I've been on, but I had no idea your relationship with J.T. was some huge secret!"

Lacey leveled an even stare at the other woman. "Then why did you make such a big deal out of my secret to begin with?"

Kelsey looked confused. "I don't know what you mean."

"Earlier in the show," Lacey explained, "you talked about someone being a fraud, about having something to hide."

An amused smile spread across the other woman's face. "That had nothing to do with you and J.T. That was about *Nate's* secret—his article, which I'd read just before you arrived."

"You mean Nate didn't tell you about me and J.T.?"

Kelsey shook her head. "Of course not."

"I don't get it. If he didn't tell you, how did you know?"

"J.T. told me," Kelsey replied. Then, obviously seeing Lacey's sudden anger, she continued. "It must have been a month ago. I'd come to meet Nate for lunch. While I waited for him, I met J.T. in the lobby. He hit on me big time."

Lacey sighed. Yes, that sounded like J.T.

"I told him I was young enough to be his daughter."

"I'll bet he loved hearing that!"

Kelsey grinned. "He almost fainted. Then he informed me that his daughter, Lacey, was definitely younger. And that you worked for him at one of his magazines. His pride was obvious."

"Oh, my gosh," Lacey said slowly.

"I never thought twice about it. It was just a casual, passing conversation. When he talked so wistfully about you during the interview, I remembered it and assumed it to be common knowledge."

Lacey mused aloud. "He never imagined it would

come back to haunt him later. He figured he could get away with bragging to a stranger." Then she remembered her last conversation with Nate. "Oh, God, what have I done?"

"Lacey, did you really think Nate had betrayed you to me?"

Placing her fingers over her mouth in horror, she nodded. "He gave me his word, and I didn't believe him."

Kelsey pursed her lips. "That's not so good."

Lacey nodded again. "He'll never forgive me."

"Sure he will," Kelsey replied with little-sister certainty. "Nate is a very forgiving kind of guy, particularly with people he loves."

"I don't know that he loves me at all," Lacey said. "I was awful to him—not only for not believing him— there's more to it than that. I think he feels I let him down."

A slow, confident smile curled across Kelsey's lips. Reaching into her diaper bag, she retrieved a manila envelope. "He loves you, Lacey. Nate left this in the studio the other night. I think you should read it."

Lacey took the envelope. "What is it?"

"It's his article. It just might have the answers you're looking for." The other woman stood. "By the way, I know Mulan's too young to be a flower girl, but I fully expect to be a bridesmaid. Purple is not my color—and I don't do taffeta."

Lacey stared in confusion as Kelsey walked away, giving her one last cheery wave. Once the other woman had gone, Lacey shut her office door, sat down behind her desk and began to read.

NATE TOOK a road trip down to Ocean City the morning after he and Lacey appeared on "Night Whispers."

He hadn't been able to sit around fighting his urge to pick up the phone and call her, or worse, waiting for her to call him.

Whatever happened with Lacey and her family situation, she had to handle it on her own. Later, when the dust settled, when and if she finally figured out his innocence, maybe she'd come back.

Back at home on Monday afternoon, Nate heard a knock on his door and padded over in bare feet to answer it. He hadn't shaved in three days and wore just a pair of sweatpants. When he opened the door, he found a delivery man holding a package.

"You Nathan Logan?"

Nate nodded and signed for the package. Grabbing a five to tip the guy, he shut the door and opened the box. "A tape?" Inside the small cardboard box was a microcassette tape, the right size to fit into his small recorder. Intrigued despite his fatigue—and his hangover—he went into his office.

Inserting the tape into his recorder, he sat down and pushed Play. Lacey's voice broke the silence of the room.

"One Woman's Battle Scars from the Sexual Revolution, by Lacey Clark."

Nate froze, listening as Lacey spoke. She was, quite obviously, reading her article aloud. He heard the shuffling of papers in the background. That made her comments all the more shocking. "You wrote this?" he asked aloud.

Her recorded voice continued. "I've written many times about true love and soul mates, about looking across a room into the eyes of the person you're destined to be with. In recent weeks, I've come to understand something—true love, perfect mates and soulful union are wonderful. But so is passion."

Nate closed his eyes, tilted his head back and continued to listen.

"How can I advise women to look for emotional compatibility when I myself have discovered my perfect man through our physical relationship? Yes, it happened backward. Yes, it's against everything I've ever believed. But it's true. Passion simply overwhelmed me. Desire wore down my resistance until I was vulnerable and open to loving him and allowing him to love me. To *awaken* me."

Nate opened his eyes, staring at the ceiling.

"There's no question I love him. I don't know what will happen next. I don't know if there will be a tomorrow, much less a happily ever after. But I do know I can no longer pretend a woman is above her passions, in control of her physical desires. I'm certainly not. I'd be a liar and a hypocrite to say I am. He controls my body and owns my soul, for as long as he wants either one of them."

On the tape, Lacey's voice continued, reading more of her article, more of the research, interview quotes and statistics. Nate had stopped listening. He no longer cared about anything else. Anything except what she'd admitted, to him on the tape, and to the world in her article.

"I love you, too, Lacey."

LACEY'S LEGS were on the verge of falling asleep as she sat in the upstairs hallway of Nate's building. She'd waited for over an hour—since the delivery man had delivered her package—for Nate to emerge. Still nothing. "Good grief, what are you doing in there?" she muttered. She'd expected—well, she'd hoped—that he'd come barreling out the door the minute he finished listening to the tape. No such luck.

Finally, when it appeared she was going to have to bite the bullet and knock on the door herself, it was yanked open.

"Hi," she whispered from her position on the floor in the hall. Nate had stepped out of his apartment, his keys in his hand, his hair damp as if he'd just emerged from the shower.

"Lacey?" He dropped to his knees beside her on the floor. "Have you been waiting long?"

She nodded. "I gave the delivery man an extra-large tip to not let on that I was here."

Grabbing her hands, he pulled her up and led her into his apartment. His eyes devoured her, yet his hands touched hers so gently. "I listened to the tape," he said.

"I read your article," she admitted.

He waited.

"I don't think my father's going to be very happy with either one of us," she continued with a tiny smile.

He threw his head back and laughed.

"Did you mean it?" she asked as he led her over to the couch and sat beside her. "What you said in the article?" She held her breath, waiting for his answer.

Smiling tenderly, he brushed his fingers across her cheek and quoted, "This journalist knows when to admit defeat. Everything I've ever believed I knew about relationships, every certainty I ever had about being above such mortal emotions as love, has dissolved under the blue-eyed stare of the woman I'd die for."

She bit her lip. "You meant it."

He continued quoting. "Sex is fun. Passion can be

consuming. But nothing, absolutely nothing, can compare to finding the other half of yourself, the partner you've been seeking since the moment you drew breath on this earth. I've been fortunate enough to find my mate. Naughty Nate is hoping to trade in his bachelor-of-the-month-club membership card for a wedding band and a minivan."

Her heart soared, but there was one more thing to say. "I'm sorry, Nate. I'm so sorry I believed you'd betrayed me. I should have trusted you, and I swear I will never doubt you again."

He tenderly cupped her face. "Forgiven. And I'm sorry if I pushed too hard, if I was callous of your parents' feelings. My only excuse is knowing how they hurt you. But I hope you know I'll support you in whatever you have to do."

There would be time later to tell him what had happened in her conversations with her mother and father. Now she was too happy to think of anything except being in his arms. "So, that minivan thing, was that kind of a proposal or something?"

"Yeah," Nate replied with a huge grin. "Whaddya say?"

She started to cry happy tears, and a laugh crossed her lips. "You sure you won't miss the wet T-shirt contests?"

"You sure you can stand a guy who'd rather tackle you on the living room floor than recite poetry beneath your balcony?"

She nodded.

Nate drew her hand to his mouth and pressed kisses on each and every finger, then moved up to sweetly kiss her lips. "This romance hero is definitely ready for his happily ever after. With you."

_____Epilogue_____

"GET ME outta here," Lacey whispered.

Nate turned his attention away from the business-man who'd been droning on for ten minutes about nothing. He glanced at his fiancée, who was fanning herself and wiping perspiration off her brow. "We're the guests of honor."

She sighed and looked around the crowded recep-tion room. Nate followed her stare, noting how similar this party was to the one the night they'd met. J.T. had insisted on inviting dozens of people to his home to celebrate Nate and Lacey's impending marriage, not to mention the huge success of their stories in this month's magazines.

"Do you really care?" Lacey finally replied, giving him a sultry look with those gorgeous blue eyes.

He didn't. Not a bit. "We might be noticed slipping away together."

"Give me ten minutes, then follow." She blew him a kiss over her shoulder as she made her way across the crowded room toward the exit.

He grinned, knowing exactly where he'd find her.

Nate supposed they should stay at the party, partic-ularly since they were leaving tomorrow for Mexico where they'd be married on a white sand beach. They'd stay for a two-week honeymoon.

A private, out-of-town wedding had seemed the saf-

est solution given the other option—having Lacey's
stepfather perform the ceremony while her real father
walked her up the aisle. Everyone had instantly nixed
that idea.

Ten minutes later, when he slipped around the
grounds and through the back door of the pool and
gym area, he immediately noticed the lighting. "Can-
dles," he murmured, following the flicker of warm
light.

"Don't fall in," she called.

He spotted her standing on the trampoline. It was a
damn good thing he'd already passed the pool, because if he'd seen her a moment earlier, he probably
would have ended up taking another unexpected
swim. "Oh, my," he murmured as he reached the edge
of the trampoline and looked at her.

She smiled at him, no shyness, no inhibition. Just
beautiful, glorious Lacey wearing a black lace push-up
bra, matching garter belt and stockings. Nothing else.

"Gee, I guess I forgot my panties altogether this
time," she said, her voice sultry and provocative.

"This works. This definitely works," Nate said when
he was finally capable of speech again, not to mention
breathing.

She started to jump, and he had to grab the metal bar
for support. Kicking off his shoes, he climbed onto the
edge of the trampoline. Then he glanced at the door
that led into the house, the one through which Lacey
had probably entered.

"I remembered to lock it," she said with a wicked
smile. Grabbing him by the tie, she pulled him onto the
bouncy surface.

"You know, I think I'm going to remember this party
better than the one at your mother's house." The en-

gagement party her mother and stepfather had thrown for them in Indiana had been pleasant, particularly with Lacey confident her mother would be okay. A few months in counseling had definitely helped that marriage, though they still had a long way to go.

She chuckled. "Me, too. Now, aren't you going to get awfully hot and sweaty jumping up here with that suit on?"

The jacket came off first, followed by the tie and the dress shirt. He stopped before reaching for his pants, noticing the way Lacey stood, one hand behind her back.

"Are you hiding something?"

"I have a little present for you," she murmured.

His heart rate kicked up as he recognized the wicked, anticipatory expression on her face.

"I was going to wait and give it to you tomorrow night in Mexico. Somehow, though, I thought we might have fun with it here tonight. Close your eyes."

He did, immediately. The trampoline shifted as she stepped closer, then Nate felt the brush of something soft and wispy against his chest. He laughed, knowing what it was.

"Think you can handle it?" she said with a saucy grin as he opened his eyes. "I've been waiting for this for months. You're sure you know what you were talking about in that article?"

He reached for the long, red feather. "Just you wait, Lacey Clark. I'm gonna make you scream."

Thankfully, J.T.'s gym was soundproof. Because Nate definitely kept his word.

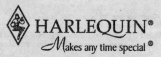

This Mother's Day Give Your Mom A Royal Treat

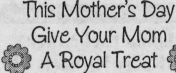

Win a fabulous one-week vacation in Puerto Rico for you and your mother at the luxurious Inter-Continental San Juan Resort & Casino. The prize includes round trip airfare for two, breakfast daily and a mother and daughter day of beauty at the beachfront hotel's spa.

INTER-CONTINENTAL
San Juan
RESORT & CASINO

Here's all you have to do:

Tell us in 100 words or less how your mother helped with the romance in your life. It may be a story about your engagement, wedding or those boyfriends when you were a teenager or any other romantic advice from your mother. The entry will be judged based on its originality, emotionally compelling nature and sincerity. See official rules on following page.

Send your entry to:
Mother's Day Contest

In Canada	**In U.S.A.**
P.O. Box 637	P.O. Box 9076
Fort Erie, Ontario	3010 Walden Ave.
L2A 5X3	Buffalo, NY
	14269-9076

Or enter online at www.eHarlequin.com

HARLEQUIN MOTHER'S DAY CONTEST 2216
OFFICIAL RULES
NO PURCHASE NECESSARY TO ENTER

Two ways to enter:

• **Via The Internet:** Log on to the Harlequin romance website (www.eHarlequin.com) anytime beginning 12:01 a.m. E.S.T., January 1, 2002 through 11:59 p.m. E.S.T., April 1, 2002 and follow the directions displayed on-line to enter your name, address (including zip code), e-mail address and in 100 words or fewer, describe how your mother helped with the romance in your life.

• **Via Mail:** Handprint (or type) on an 8 1/2" x 11" plain piece of paper, your name, address (including zip code) and e-mail address (if you have one), and in 100 words or fewer, describe how your mother helped with the romance in your life. Mail your entry via first-class mail to: Harlequin Mother's Day Contest 2216, (in the U.S.) P.O. Box 9076, Buffalo, NY 14269-9076; (in Canada) P.O. Box 637, Fort Erie, Ontario, Canada L2A 5X3.

For eligibility, entries must be submitted either through a completed Internet transmission or postmarked no later than 11:59 p.m. E.S.T., April 1, 2002 (mail-in entries must be received by April 9, 2002). Limit one entry per person, household address and e-mail address. On-line and/or mailed entries received from persons residing in geographic areas in which entry is not permissible will be disqualified.

Entries will be judged by a panel of judges, consisting of members of the Harlequin editorial, marketing and public relations staff using the following criteria:
- Originality - 50%
- Emotional Appeal - 25%
- Sincerity - 25%

In the event of a tie, duplicate prizes will be awarded. Decisions of the judges are final.

Prize: A 6-night/7-day stay for two at the Inter-Continental San Juan Resort & Casino, including round-trip coach air transportation from gateway airport nearest winner's home (approximate retail value: $4,000). Prize includes breakfast daily and a mother and daughter day of beauty at the beachfront hotel's spa. Prize consists of only those items listed as part of the prize. Prize is valued in U.S. currency.

All entries become the property of Torstar Corp. and will not be returned. No responsibility is assumed for lost, late, illegible, incomplete, inaccurate, non-delivered or misdirected mail or misdirected e-mail, for technical, hardware or software failures of any kind, lost or unavailable network connections, or failed, incomplete, garbled or delayed computer transmission or any human error which may occur in the receipt or processing of the entries in this Contest.

Contest open only to residents of the U.S. (except Colorado) and Canada, who are 18 years of age or older and is void wherever prohibited by law; all applicable laws and regulations apply. Any litigation within the Province of Quebec respecting the conduct or organization of a publicity contest may be submitted to the Régie des alcools, des courses et des jeux for a ruling. Any litigation respecting the awarding of a prize may be submitted to the Régie des alcools, des courses et des jeux only for the purpose of helping the parties reach a settlement. Employees and immediate family members of Torstar Corp. and D.L. Blair, Inc., their affiliates, subsidiaries and all other agencies, entities and persons connected with the use, marketing or conduct of this Contest are not eligible to enter. Taxes on prize are the sole responsibility of winner. Acceptance of any prize offered constitutes permission to use winner's name, photograph or other likeness for the purposes of advertising, trade and promotion on behalf of Torstar Corp., its affiliates and subsidiaries without further compensation to the winner, unless prohibited by law.

Winner will be determined no later than April 15, 2002 and be notified by mail. Winner will be required to sign and return an Affidavit of Eligibility form within 15 days after winner notification. Non-compliance within that time period may result in disqualification and an alternate winner may be selected. Winner of trip must execute a Release of Liability prior to ticketing and must possess required travel documents (e.g. Passport, photo ID) where applicable. Travel must be completed within 12 months of selection and is subject to traveling companion completing and returning a Release of Liability prior to travel; and hotel and flight accommodations availability. Certain restrictions and blackout dates may apply. No substitution of prize permitted by winner. Torstar Corp. and D.L. Blair, Inc., their parents, affiliates, and subsidiaries are not responsible for errors in printing or electronic presentation of Contest, or entries. In the event of printing or other errors which may result in unintended prize values or duplication of prizes, all affected entries shall be null and void. If for any reason the Internet portion of the Contest is not capable of running as planned, including infection by computer virus, bugs, tampering, unauthorized intervention, fraud, technical failures, or any other causes beyond the control of Torstar Corp. which corrupt or affect the administration, secrecy, fairness, integrity or proper conduct of the Contest, Torstar Corp. reserves the right, at its sole discretion, to disqualify any individual who tampers with the entry process and to cancel, terminate, modify or suspend the Contest or the Internet portion thereof. In the event the Internet portion must be terminated a notice will be posted on the website and all entries received prior to termination will be judged in accordance with these rules. In the event of a dispute regarding an on-line entry, the entry will be deemed submitted by the authorized holder of the e-mail account submitted at the time of entry. Authorized account holder is defined as the natural person who is assigned to an e-mail address by an Internet access provider, on-line service provider or other organization that is responsible for arranging e-mail address for the domain associated with the submitted e-mail address. Torstar Corp. and/or D.L. Blair Inc. assumes no responsibility for any computer injury or damage related to or resulting from accessing and/or downloading any sweepstakes material. Rules are subject to any requirements/limitations imposed by the FCC. **Purchase or acceptance of a product offer does not improve your chances of winning.**

For winner's name (available after May 1, 2002), send a self-addressed, stamped envelope to: Harlequin Mother's Day Contest Winners 2216, P.O. Box 4200 Blair, NE 68009-4200 or you may access the www.eHarlequin.com Web site through June 3, 2002.

Contest sponsored by Torstar Corp., P.O. Box 9042, Buffalo, NY 14269-9042.

If you enjoyed what you just read,
then we've got an offer you can't resist!

Take 2 bestselling
love stories FREE!

Plus get a FREE surprise gift!

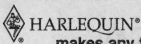

Every day is

A Mother's Day

in this heartwarming anthology
celebrating motherhood and romance!

Featuring the classic story "Nobody's Child" by Emilie Richards
He had come to a child's rescue, and now Officer Farrell Riley was
suddenly sharing parenthood with beautiful Gemma Hancock.
But would their ready-made family last forever?

Plus two brand-new romances:

"Baby on the Way" by Marie Ferrarella
Single and pregnant, Madeline Reed found the perfect husband in the
handsome cop who helped bring her infant son into the world. But did his
dutiful role in the surprise delivery make J. T. Walker a daddy?

"A Daddy for Her Daughters" by Elizabeth Bevarly
When confronted with spirited Naomi Carmichael and her brood of girls,
bachelor Sloan Sullivan realized he had a lot to learn about women!
Especially if he hoped to win this sexy single mom's heart....

Available this April from Silhouette Books!

Where love comes alive™

These New York Times *bestselling authors*
have created stories to capture the hearts and minds
of women everywhere.
Here are three classic tales about the power of love—
and the wonder of discovering the place
where you belong....

FINDING HOME

DUNCAN'S BRIDE
by
LINDA HOWARD

CHAIN LIGHTNING
by
ELIZABETH LOWELL

POPCORN AND KISSES
by
KASEY MICHAELS

Available only from Silhouette
at your favorite retail outlet.

Silhouette®
Where love comes alive™

Visit Silhouette at www.eHarlequin.com   PSFH